"Let's start here…"

Jonas's lips were soft, responsive, warm. Allie closed her eyes to concentrate on their shape, their taste, the change between the moist curves of his mouth and the smooth skin of his cheeks and chin, delivers through her bo

He let her k   heir movements.   the power associa   and connections, was leaving Little Brooklyn Allie in control.

Very gradually she started to rock back and forth over the thin fabric of his shorts, continuing to explore his mouth without kissing him full on or deeply. *Always hold something back.*

Jonas inhaled through his teeth. Allie let her head drop back, riding him, eyes still closed, taking her pleasure.

"Allie." He'd bent forward, murmured against her throat. "You're making me crazy."

You're making me crazy, too.

She had to work harder and harder to appear calm. Her breath caught in little gasps and her thighs began to tremble. Not the plan. Not what wa

To

Isabel Sharpe was not born pen in hand, like so many of her fellow writers. After she quit work to stay home with her firstborn son and nearly went out of her mind, she started writing. After more than thirty novels, a second son, and eventually a new, improved husband, Isabel is more than happy with her choices these days.

She loves hearing from readers. Write to her at www.isabelsharpe.com

Recent titles by the same author:

MY WILDEST RIDE
INDULGE ME
NO HOLDING BACK
WHILE SHE WAS SLEEPING…

**Did you know these are also available as eBooks?
Visit www.millsandboon.co.uk**

NOTHING TO HIDE

BY
ISABEL SHARPE

MILLS & BOON

Published in Great Britain 2014
by Mills & Boon, an imprint of Harlequin (UK) Limited,
Eton House, 18-24 Paradise Road, Richmond, Surrey, TW9 1SR

© 2013 Muna Shehadi Sill

ISBN: 978-0-263-90918-0

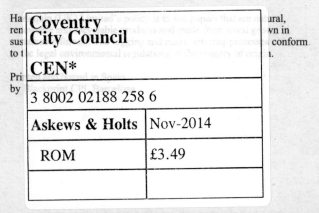

Coventry City Council CEN*	
3 8002 02188 258 6	
Askews & Holts	Nov-2014
ROM	£3.49

NOTHING TO HIDE

To my wonderful new brothers and sisters-in-law,
John and Nicky, David and Mary, Matt and Lisa,
and Seth and Bridie.

You couldn't have made me feel more welcome to the family.

CHAPTER ONE

"I STILL CAN'T believe I was fired. Everyone loved my work. They told me so every day. Well, okay, most days." Allie McDonald paced from one end of her and Julie's living room to the other, which took about four and a half steps. You had to love the wide-open spaces of Manhattan apartments. She could pace the kitchen standing still. "Clients loved my ideas, too. I heard a hundred times how their products or services really popped in the pieces I designed. And most of all, it makes no sense that they'd let *me* go and keep old whatshername, who everyone hated, even though she's been there forever."

"Yeah?" Her roommate sedately turned a page of *Saveur* magazine, her long legs tucked under her on their bright red couch. "Get over it."

"I know, I know, you're sick of me." Allie stopped pacing and shoved her hands through her long hair. Her bangs were getting caught on her eyelashes. At least she could hack those off herself. The rest could just keep growing until she got another job. With luck she wouldn't look like Rapunzel by then. "I've been whining about this for the past week."

"Have you?" Julie turned another page, examining it with apparent fascination. "Honestly, I stopped listening after the first four or five hundred times."

Allie cracked up. A native New Yorker through and through, Julie Turner talked tough but she'd walk through lava to help those she loved. They'd been roommates and fast friends at the Rhode Island School of Design—Allie with a full scholarship, Julie with a full tuition check from Mom and Dad—and had found this apartment through one of Julie's parents' friends. No matter what you needed or wanted in the city, the Turners knew someone or knew someone who knew someone.

It would be very easy to hate Julie if she wasn't so wonderful. Beautiful, sophisticated, wealthy and smart, she led a charmed life. Men fell for her in droves. She could eat whatever she wanted and stay thin. Straight out of RISD, she'd landed a job at *Vanity Fair*…

Come to think of it, Julie was the type of woman Allie's father had ditched his family for. Only Julie was human.

Allie wasn't the type men lined up for. She had dull caramel-blond hair and girl-next-door features, scoured secondhand shops, made her own clothes and controlled her weight through relentless exercise and constant sacrifice. It took her nearly a year after graduating to land her job as a graphic artist at Boynton Advertising. Five years later, having been promoted to assistant art director, the company hit hard times and—bang, thanks, bye— here she was, pounding the crowded New York City pavement *again,* worrying about rent *again,* though Julie had promised to cover her until Allie got back on her feet. Trust funds must be wonderful things. The closest Allie ever got to a trust fund was the jar in their old Brooklyn apartment into which her mother dropped quarters whenever Allie babysat her five brothers and managed not to kill any of them.

She flopped onto the couch next to Julie and let her head sink back on the cushion. "I feel like a failure."

"You're not a failure."

"I didn't say I was a failure, I said I felt like one."

"Stop feeling like a failure."

Allie clapped her hands. "Hey, that worked. Thanks!"

"Your problem is that you don't have enough to do."

"Because I have no job, because I was *fired.*"

Julie snorted. "You're doing everything you're supposed to be doing to find another one. But it's not enough to fill your day, so you—"

"Get restless and cranky and then I whine at you."

"Yuh-huh." Julie put down her magazine. "Hey, you know I don't mind. Whine away. God knows I would. Losing your job is serious stuff. As I've said over and over, if there's anything I can do to help, let me know. Besides giving you my job."

"Aw! I was just about to ask for it." Allie grinned at her. "You are doing more than enough just putting up with me. This is so not where I thought I'd be six years out of school."

Julie lifted a perfect dark eyebrow. "My *point* is you need something to do, some project. Like design a line of clothing that will take London, Paris and Milan by storm. You'll fill your time and your creative well."

"My creative well." Allie stared hopelessly at a triangular crack in the ceiling paint. She hadn't designed anything substantive since she'd started working at Boynton. "Someone threw a plagued rat into it."

"There's my little optimist."

Allie's cell phone rang from her back pocket. She pulled it out. Maybe a job interview? Maybe London, Paris or Milan?

"It's *Erik*."

"Oooh, your favorite colleague and sexual predator."

"Ex-colleague. Who finally did stop hitting on me."

"Because you're not there anymore."

"Good point." Allie answered the call. "Hey, Erik."

"Alli-i-ie." He yelled her name so loudly Allie yanked the phone from her ear. Julie rolled her eyes and went back to her magazine.

"Shhh, Erik. Jeez, you just made my head explode."

"And that's a problem because…"

"What's going on? No!" She raised her hand dramatically. "Don't tell me. Boynton wants me back. They're begging, in fact."

"They should be. They're morons for letting you go."

Even though Erik tended to say whatever people wanted to hear, she decided this time he was being absolutely sincere. "They certainly are."

"So how are you doing?"

"Anxious. Frustrated. Bored."

"Need a little excitement?"

"Uhh…why don't you tell me what kind of excitement first, then I'll tell you if I need it." A lead on a job was the kind of excitement she needed. Erik trying to get into her pants was not.

Getting into female pants was what Erik did. If he could get women to pay him for sex, he'd be twice the billionaire he already was, due to family megabucks. Sometimes she thought the only reason he paid her so much attention was because he still hadn't succeeded with her. Nor would he ever, which she'd told him in no uncertain terms, but to Erik that was so much blah-blah-blah.

The funny thing was, Allie liked him. Really liked him. She respected that he worked hard at a day job like the rest of the poor rats in the race. And she suspected that underneath all the BS and swagger there was an insecure mess of a guy with a really good heart. She even managed to feel a little sorry for him. Which meant she was nice to him, which, unfortunately, meant he thought he still had a chance. Men were pretty slow about stuff like that.

"This is the chance of a lifetime, Allie."

"Uh-huh."

"How'd you like to spend a week in the Adirondacks on Lake George? Or two weeks?"

"Your family's summer house?" She'd heard about the place and had seen a few pictures—beautiful house, beautiful lake. The temptation was immediate, even as she was formulating her no-thank-you speech. Leave hot, smelly New York in July for a luxury oasis? For a wonderfully cool, breezy, relaxing week…or two? It would be impractical, irresponsible, and serve as needless encouragement for the Great Horned Predator, but who wouldn't be tempted?

"Yes, our cottage in the woods."

Allie snorted. If that enormous place was a cottage, she was the queen of planet earth. "So, Erik, we're talking a week up there, just the two of us?"

Julie shook her head emphatically no.

"Oh. Well… Wait, I haven't gotten to the best part."

"I'm listening." She was a little afraid of the best part.

"My grandmother and great-grandmother were total fashionistas and they never threw anything away. The attic is full of their clothes. In mint condition."

Allie came to full attention. Antique clothes. Her passion. "Really."

"Here's the best part. Mom wants to get rid of them before we sell the house."

"You're *selling* that place?"

"Yeah." His voice thickened. "Since Mom and Dad moved to Germany they can't get back here often enough to make it worthwhile. I've been after my brother to buy it with me, but so far no good. I'd buy it myself, but it's too much for one person to keep up. And they're right, the house deserves to be used and lived in."

"Erik, that's terrible." She knew how much he loved the place.

"It is. But back to the clothes. There are at least four trunks. You'll get first rights to everything."

"I'll— *Everything?*" Allie stood there, blinking at Julie's curious stare. Erik's grandmother and great-grandmother would mean clothes from the 1920s and '40s. This could be an amazing collection. It could be fashion nirvana. "Wow. That sounds incredible. But, Erik…it'll just be you and me up there?"

Julie waggled her finger urgently, no, no, no.

"Allie, Allie, Allie. You still don't trust me?"

"Nuh-uh," she said pleasantly, her heart still pounding at the thought of all those clothes. Would she sell her body for this chance?

Umm…not quite.

"I'm not going to try anything. I swear." He was trying very hard to sound sincere. Or maybe he *was* sincere. It was frustratingly hard to tell with Erik. "I figured you'd want first shot at the clothes. Plus, you being in a tough spot and all, I thought the break would be nice, too."

"I don't know…"

Julie drew her finger across her neck. Cut!

"Yeah, so, anyway." Erik cleared his throat. "It won't be just me there."

Allie narrowed her eyes. "Now you're telling me this?"

"Yeah. Yeah."

She waited. Nothing. "So…who else will be there?"

Julie frowned skeptically.

"My brother, Jonas. And his girlfriend."

Hmm. Allie narrowed her eyes, ignoring the jump in her pulse at the mention of his brother, the hottest man in the Northeast if not the universe. "Are you making this up?"

"*No,* I'm not making this up. What makes you think I'm making this up?"

"The way you never hesitate to make things up."

"I'll prove it to you. I'll have Jonas email you saying he's going. That okay?"

"I'm not even sure *I'm* going."

"How could you not go? A whole attic full of clothes, Allie, yours for the taking. Gowns and hats and shoes and I don't know, they probably even kept underwear. How can you pass this up?"

She didn't think she could. Not only would the break do her good, but somewhere in this treasure trove of history, there might be the seeds of a new business or career. All her life she'd been obsessed with clothes of the past, watched old movies obsessively, worshipped Edith Head, who'd costumed the greatest stars from the golden age of cinema—the 1920s to the 1960s. When Allie was a little girl, she'd designed outfits for her dolls on her mom's old sewing machine, and started designing her own clothes in high school.

Reality hit her when she graduated from college. She needed a stable, well-paying career, because unlike Erik, she couldn't count on her family for support or inheritance. Three of her five brothers had gone to community colleges to learn trades, but Allie had wanted more from the minute she was old enough to understand the difference between the haves and have-nots. Which, not coincidentally, was when her father had met La Richesse Bitchesse and left them to live on the Upper East Side. He'd moved into a fabulous full-floor condo with his new wife and her two snotty kids, while his real family had moved to Kensington in Brooklyn. All seven of them had crammed into a three-bedroom apartment located in a borderline neighborhood at best. Mom had started drinking in earnest then.

A few times a year they visited their father in his luxury digs, and were sneered at by his new children and ignored by his wife, Betsy. Allie had vowed that someday she'd live well enough to get back at him for what he'd done to them. And that she'd never make the same mistake her mother had, and depend on a man for her livelihood. Nor would she make the same mistake her father had, and go crawling after money she hadn't earned.

"I'll pick you up on Friday after work."

"Erik…"

"Jonas will be emailing you as soon as I can get in touch with him."

"Erik."

Julie threw up her hands.

"We'll have fun. More than fun. We'll have a blast. And you'll come back with a truckload of the most fabulous clothes you've ever seen."

"I haven't decided yet." Except she sort of had.

"C'mon, say you'll go." Mr. Account Executive, trying to close the sale.

"Give me an hour to think about it."

"Allie, Allie, you *want* to go, you know you want to go. You can keep up with job openings online, you have your cell in case anyone calls, you're mere hours away if you need to get back. You won't miss anything. Unless you stay here."

He was right. Her panic stemmed from feeling as if she could control her life better from here, where the solutions lay. But really, she could stay on top of the job hunt up in paradise, too. If any of the résumés she'd sent out caught someone's eye, Allie could rush home in a blink.

In the meantime, there were those clothes. And that lake. And the elegant house. Julie's life. Her father's life. Maybe hers someday. Lives that fascinated as much as they repelled her. Just for a week. Or two. Then back to reality and more important things.

"You absolutely promise your brother will be there with his girlfriend, and that this is not some elaborate seduction ploy?"

"I absolutely promise." He spoke firmly, without hesitation.

Allie turned away from Julie's warning look. "Okay, Erik. I'll go."

JONAS SAT IN the conference room at Boston Consulting, tapping his capped pen on his thigh. Same old meeting, same old client, same old problems. Same old management consulting team suggesting the same old solutions. Give the employees a suggestion box. Combine a few positions into one. Develop more efficient means of bringing the product to market by reorganizing the physical space and eliminating redundant steps.

Yeah. That would help slow down, possibly reverse, the slide the company was in right now. For today, tomorrow, next year, the year after that. It would be good enough, stop the worst of the bleeding. But to become one of the future leaders of the industry, they'd have to do more. Make harder choices, shake up corporate culture to a degree that would panic everyone, at least for a while. When the changes took hold, when employees could walk into the building not just with an absence of bitterness and dread, but with a real sense of team spirit and enthusiasm, *then* BC would have really done its job.

But Boston Consulting execs didn't think that way. Jonas knew that, because once he rose through the ranks of consultants to a level where he had the power to make recommendations, he'd made several, all of which he'd been excited about, all of which would have meant real progress for the companies they served, real progress for them. But he'd been shot down every time.

Too expensive. Jonas, the client is looking for us to save money, not spend more.

Too radical. It will never fly.

Jonas was thinking more and more that he didn't belong there.

Yeah, okay, he'd been thinking that for the past year, and he still hadn't done anything about it. The first six months, he'd been a basket case after breaking up with Missy. The next six months… he had no excuse but his own passivity.

The meeting droned on. Jonas's pen tapped harder. He maintained his expression of interest, automatically turning toward whoever was speaking, but took in only enough that if his opinion were asked, he'd be able to contribute coherently. Automatic pilot. Robo-employee.

He wanted out of there.

As if God had heard his prayer, his cell phone started vibrating. Erik. Immediately he got up, waving his phone apologetically at the stony faces in the room, and bolted. *Very important call. Have to go. So sorry. If it wasn't urgent...*

"Hey, Erik, what's up?"

"I need you to come to Lake George this weekend. And all of next week. And maybe the week after that."

Jonas gave a brief laugh. His brother shouldn't be able to surprise him anymore, but he still managed. "Yeah? What for?"

"Allie McDonald."

"What about her?" He'd met Allie last December. He'd joined her and Erik for dinner when he'd been in New York on business. She'd been different from the artificial blondes Erik usually went after—Allie had seemed more genuine. She had the same sophistication, intelligence and beauty of Erik's girlfriends, but it hadn't seemed as if she'd been trying to impress anyone. Jonas remembered that night as a landmark: it was when he'd really begun to believe that he'd survive Missy's betrayal. "You're still dating her?"

"Still trying to."

"Still *trying* over six months later? Is this a record?" It was beyond him how his brother scored with as many women as he did. Jonas's theory was that he wore them down by being so persistently charming that they eventually gave in, hoping he'd leave them alone. But this was a new level of chase.

"Allie's different."

"Uh-huh." Behind him, the meeting door opened. Jonas strode down the hall toward his office so his team wouldn't realize his important call had to do with whether or not his brother could get laid. "Different because she's turned you down longer than anyone else?"

"This trip to Lake George is my best chance yet. I think she's weakening."

"Really." Jonas pushed open the door of his office. Ten years with the company and he finally had a door, which at times he was very happy to be able to close. "Then why do you want *me* there?"

"I promised you'd be around. To chaperone."

"*That's* your best chance? With a woman who doesn't want to be alone with you?"

"She agreed to spend the week with me, didn't she?"

"Uh, yeah." Jonas pinched the bridge of his nose between his fingers. He was developing a headache named Erik. His brother's life was a restless and relentless quest for a type of fulfillment Jonas was convinced Erik hadn't yet identified, which obviously didn't stop him from trying to achieve it. Erik changed styles, cars, apartments, jobs and women as if nothing held his attention for longer than a season. He drove their steady, regimented German father completely up a wall. Sometimes Jonas thought Mom and Dad had moved to Munich not only to care for Dad's parents, but so they wouldn't have to watch their younger son play hummingbird through his life.

"I'm doing us both a favor. She got laid off."

"Tough break." He went to his window—with a view of the building next door—and pictured Allie sitting across from him at the restaurant, cheeks pink from the wine, hazel eyes bright under girlish wheat-colored bangs, talking about her design-career hopes and ambitions with every ounce of the passion he no longer had for his. Being laid off would have hit her hard. That depth of excitement had been one of the sexiest things about her.

What he hadn't seen in Allie was even the slightest trace of sexual interest in his brother. Unless Jonas's radar had misfired, he'd say he had more chemistry with her than Erik did, though a lot could've changed in seven months. Was she really "weakening"—Erik's typically charming choice of words? It was disappointing to think she might fall like the rest of them.

"She's incredibly talented. You should see the costume designs she did in school. I told her about Grandma Bridget and Great-Grandma Josephine's clothes and how Mom wants to get rid of them. She was practically drooling."

Aha. So Allie could be more interested in the clothes than his brother. Jonas relaxed his shoulders, unaware of how tightly he'd been holding them.

"So you'll come?"

"Erik, I can't just take a week off work."

"Sure you can. You just don't think you should."

Jonas suppressed a jolt of irritation and tapped a pencil on his desk. His brother always made him out to be a somber slave to duty like their father. Maybe compared with Erik's hedonistic lifestyle he was the more responsible one, but nothing extreme, and typical for an oldest child.

He *could* go up for the weekend. It had been a while since he'd been to Lake George. Two years, since the last time the family got together there before his parents' move.

"A long weekend, then," Erik said.

"Quite a drive for a weekend."

"C'mon, help me out, brother."

Jonas rolled his eyes. He usually did give in to his brother, sometimes against his own instinct. But Erik was family, and that seemed to win out. Jonas rarely asked for anything in return—but there was one thing he did want from his brother now. "Tell you what. I'll go up for a long weekend if you drop your objections to selling the house."

There was a long silence. Jonas had expected an immediate refusal. Either Erik had been considering changing his mind anyway, or he wanted this time with Allie more than Jonas thought. "For that, you'd owe me a whole week."

Jonas peered at his BlackBerry, checking the next week's schedule. He could move his Monday trip to Wednesday afternoon and take Monday and Tuesday off.

"Half a week. I'd have to leave Wednesday morning."

"Deal."

Jonas lowered his brows suspiciously. His brother had been persistently vocal in his objections to selling Morningside. "Just like that?"

"Look, you, Mom and Dad all want to sell. I'm outnumbered, I get that. This is sooner than I'd planned to cave, but I'll do it for Allie."

"Okay." The victory left Jonas less triumphant than he'd expected. With their parents abroad, the house had been sitting empty except for Erik's brief, infrequent visits. Upkeep was expensive. With money from the sale of the house, Jonas would rather buy a retreat of his own, closer to Boston, maybe in Cape Cod. A place he could use year-round.

"Bring Sandra."

"Jeez, Erik."

"I told Allie—"

"Well, un-tell her. I'm not involving Sandra in your schemes."

"This isn't a scheme. I think Allie could be the one."

Jonas turned from the window. He'd never heard Erik talk like that. Size of boobs, lushness of ass, depth of sexual depravity, sure, but *marriage?* "You're kidding."

"I'm not kidding. I'm crazy about her. She's everything I want."

"Since when do you want to get married?"

"I'm almost thirty. It's time. And I want kids."

Jonas took the phone and stared at it before replacing it to his ear. "Who are you, and what have you done with my brother?"

"Just call Sandra."

"She'll have shows this weekend."

"So have her come next week."

Jonas scowled, tempted in spite of himself. Sandra was a long-ago lover and good friend. She'd been a rock during the ugly breakup with Missy. "You're a piece of work."

"I owe you one, bro."

Jonas hung up the phone, shaking his head. He could stand up to the highest-level executives in the company. But around his brother he became as indulgent as their grandfather, who used to bring cookies and candy from Germany when he visited, as if Jonas and Erik were still kids. Really *good* cookies and candy. They didn't object.

Taking consolation from the knowledge that if he didn't want to make the trip to Lake George, wild horses couldn't make him, he dialed Sandra, whom he'd known for ten years, since the night he'd gone to one of her shows on a musician friend's suggestion. She'd spotted him in the audience and had come over to his table. They spent the intermission together, then time after the show, then made a long, hot night of it—that night and several others. For two years, if they weren't seeing other people, they'd hook up for a night, once a week, sometimes more, sometimes less. He'd liked the uncomplicated nature of their sexual relationship and was disappointed when she ended it and broke off contact. Happily, they met again by chance a few years later, and had started a platonic friendship. Who knew, maybe they would end up together forever. They joked about it now and then.

Sandra picked up. "Hey, hottie, what's happening?"

"Want to come with me to Lake George for a long weekend?"

She gasped theatrically. "Oh, you are *so* speaking my language."

"Seriously? You don't have a show?"

"I'm between them, and can't stand myself anymore. You called just as I was about to become a heroin and shopping-channel addict. I don't know which one's worse."

"Yeah?" He chuckled. She had a fairly edgy sense of humor, to put it mildly. Came from a rough childhood in South Boston. "Put down the needle and the remote and pack your bags."

"When do we leave?"

"Considering the week I'm having, not soon enough. Saturday morning? I have a dinner meeting Friday."

She clucked her tongue. "Only you would have a business meeting on a Friday night."

"He's a client in town for a conference."

"I'm telling you, they own your very fine Jon-ass."

"Ha." He bristled at the dig. "Maybe not for long."

"Yeah?" She dropped the sensual lounge singer act she did so well, her voice rising to its normal sweet pitch. "No offense, but I've been hearing that for a while."

Jonas sighed wearily. "I know. But I'm getting closer. We can talk."

"Good deal. Saturday suits me fine. What brought this on, by the way? I thought you were going to get rid of the place."

"We've been summoned to chaperone young Erik and his latest target."

"*Erik* needs a chaperone? What's wrong with that boy? Or more to the point, what's wrong with the woman? Frigid? Closet gay? From a past century?"

"I was just asking him the same thing. Between you and me, I think it's a case of 'she's just not that into him.'"

"Ah. I suppose even a master can fail sometimes. Well, after all the stories you've told me, I look forward to watching him in action."

"That makes one of us." His voice came out more brusquely than he intended. "I'm sure he can't teach *you* a thing."

"You got that right." Her voice went back to the sensual purr she used in her act to great effect. Sandra had been performing since she could walk, in community theater, in equity shows and her favorite—singing jazz and show tunes in clubs around Boston. She was beautiful, sexy, magnetic and a hell of a singer. "I also look forward to hanging out with you, Jonas."

"That definitely makes two of us." He hung up the phone, still annoyed with Erik and with himself for being persuaded, but now thinking the weekend might be just what he needed. A chance to get away, gain some perspective on life and work and what he wanted to do next. Lake George was a good place for that kind of deep thinking. And he'd have the chance to catch up with an old friend.

Nothing strange about that. He always looked forward to seeing Sandra. The odd thing was his immediate follow-up thought: that he was also looking forward to seeing Allie.

CHAPTER TWO

Hi Allie,

Erik asked me to email you to confirm that I'll be at Lake George on Saturday (the 19th)—he didn't think you believed I was coming. Obviously you're a smart woman. I'll make sure he behaves, though I'm guessing you can take care of yourself.

By the way, sorry you got laid off. The world makes no sense sometimes. I'm sure you'll find a job soon. Mine isn't thrilling me these days—I'm dreaming about starting my own company.

Wow. I haven't admitted that to anyone yet. Barely even to myself. So now you know my deepest secret.

Jonas

P.S. It will be good to see you again. I enjoyed meeting you in New York

Hey Jonas,

No, I probably won't need your protection, but I also enjoyed meeting you last Christmas. Erik said you're bringing your girlfriend. Was he telling the truth there, too?

Thanks for the sympathy on being laid off. I'm sure something else will turn up. It's the limbo that's hard. Luckily I've had every crap job a teenager can land, so I won't starve.

As for your new company, congratulations! But if that's your deepest secret, you need more excitement.

Allie

Hi Allie,

I'm bringing an old friend. Sandra.

As for needing more excitement, hmm. Maybe being back at Lake George will inspire me to wilder things?

On that note, why are you stuck vacationing with Erik? I would think there'd be an army of Manhattan men clawing for your at-

tention. Or do you just turn them all down? You should come to
Boston. It's a great city.
Jonas

Hey Jonas,
Ha! The only men clawing for my attention want me to pay my
bills. As for Boston, you're seriously tempting me.
Allie

I bet you say that to all the guys.
Jonas

Only the ones who do.
Allie

ALLIE CLIMBED OUT of Erik's Mercedes after a long, bumpy ride
down a tree-lined gravel driveway branching off a road halfway
up the west side of Lake George. She inhaled the light, cool air
with relief, having spent too many miles listening to Erik's horrible music.

The Meyers' property and Morningside—really, they named
their house?—were even more stately and elegant in person than
they'd looked in the pictures Erik showed her. Determined not
to betray her intimidation or awe, Allie dragged her suitcase out
of the backseat, waving off the very solicitous Erik who'd come
around to help. He was being the perfect gentleman—almost too
perfect. Less like a concerned friend and more like a guy lull-
ing his intended victim into complacency. On the way over, he'd
taken her to a lovely bistro off Interstate 87, and had seemed a
little too eager to refill her wineglass, a little too eager to compliment her, touch her arm, bump hands and shoulders when they
were walking. Maybe she was paranoid, but her guard was up—
to put it mildly—and she was very glad Jonas and Sandra would
be arriving the next day.

Jonas, anyway. Sandra, not so much.

Stop! Honestly, one meeting last Christmas and a few emails
and she was as giddy as a preteen with a crush, obsessing over

every word he'd said. Allie was the only person he'd told about wanting to start his own company? Uh-huh. Did she remember whose brother he was? Boston was probably littered with women who were "the only person he'd told."

Shutting down those thoughts, she turned to face Morningside, which was lit with a soft glow from outdoor lights and the moon. The place was imposing. Eight bedrooms, Erik had said, in two gleaming white stories. A wide screened-in porch—or should she say a ver-*an*-da—wrapped around the north side, punctuated by a white balustrade and a lattice fence that effectively hid unsightly underparts. The south end of the house, also two stories, sat slightly lower, like a stunted afterthought. Black shutters—Dark green? Navy? Hard to tell at night—downstairs, and on the second floor, dormers relieved the whiteness. Farther north on the property and closer to the lake was the silhouette of a smaller house, begging to be explored. By the water stood a third structure, a boathouse, she'd guess. Surrounding the family compound, a fern-strewn pine and hardwood forest covered hills that came right to the water's edge on either side of the curving sand beach. The grass around the house looked freshly mowed. She wouldn't be surprised if the sand by the lake had been raked, too. The place had been thoroughly readied for the Lord of the Manor's visit.

Sarcasm aside, Morningside was tranquil and totally private. Allie was glad that she wouldn't have to cope with a cluster of mansions, women twirling parasols, wearing bonnets and the latest frocks, their gold-plated opera glasses trained on Allie, anticipating her every faux pas.

Okay, wrong century, but real fears.

From an early age she'd been conscious of class status in a way no one else in her blue-collar family seemed to be. Not that she'd grown up in the jungle, though at times Brooklyn felt that wild. But she'd been the only one of her siblings so determined to put that life behind her. Which she had. Just not *this* far.

"You like it?" Erik's blue eyes were bright with pleasure, or maybe just reflecting the moonlight.

"How could I not?" She gestured to the house and grounds,

acting as if this was just the latest in the long line of similar vacation mansions she'd stayed in. "It's beautiful. So quiet."

"C'mon, I'll show you inside. You can have Mom's room upstairs."

She fell in step beside him on the flagstone path. "And where do you sleep?"

"I'll be in Dad's room." His voice was casual. "There's a connecting door, but you can lock it if you're worried."

Allie stopped walking. "How many keys?"

"Allie, Allie, Allie." He bent to take her suitcase up the front steps. "You have nothing to fear from me."

Said the shark to the seal. "If you say so."

"I do. Jonas and Sandra will be here tomorrow. They're sleeping down the hall and will hear your screams of terror and revulsion if I attack you."

"Uh, yeah, thanks, Erik, that helps a lot." She gestured toward the small cottage out back. "So what's that place, the butler's quarters?"

"Nah. Escape pod, used by various people over the generations. Mom had sleepovers there with girlfriends. I think my grandparents honeymooned there. Jonas slept there when he was a teenager. My great-grandfather used it most. He was a writer with five kids and needed peace and quiet."

"How nice for your great-grandmother that *he* had somewhere to go." She rolled her eyes, imagining the poor woman managing five screeching kids while her husband peacefully awaited inspiration.

Erik dismissed her with a wave. "They probably had one nanny for each kid. Great-Grandma Josephine was a party animal. Wait till you see her outfits."

"I can't wait."

"Tomorrow." He unlocked the front door. "The light will be better up in the attic."

Inside, the house was cool and still, but with none of the mustiness one would expect from a place shut up for so long. Erik hit a switch and a brass chandelier sprang to light, illuminating the tiled foyer and curving staircase ascending to the left. To the right, against the wall under a huge gilt-framed mirror, stood a glass table on which sat a low vase of perfectly dried flowers—lavender, hydrangea, roses and curly willow.

Glimpses into the surrounding rooms revealed similar decor. Subtle, simple, nothing overdone. Everything reeked of elegance and good taste. Julie had that talent. She could absently throw on skinny pants and any old shirt and look ten times more chic than Allie trying her hardest. Dad's wife, Betsy, was the same way, only she was openly smug about it.

Maybe the gift of effortless style came with the money genes.

"It's late, I'm beat." Erik gave a long, loud yawn. "I'll treat you to the full tour tomorrow, if that's okay."

"Sure, no problem." Allie followed him up the staircase, hiding her oh-so-low-class disappointment. She felt like a little kid, wanting to see everything *now!* The downstairs, the upstairs, the cottage, the boathouse. She wanted to take a long moonlit walk by the lake, lie on the beach and count stars…

But okay, she'd still be here tomorrow night, and several more after that. She'd get her moonlit walk, probably more than once.

Upstairs, the landing was furnished with a grandfather clock and old-fashioned daybed. Near a window overlooking the lake were a smaller wing chair and a bookcase. It was a perfect spot for a rainy day.

"Yours." Turning right down a long hall, Erik pushed open the first door on the lake side and ushered Allie in.

"Wow." She walked to the center of the good-size room and turned slowly, taking it all in. The bed was the centerpiece: a white iron frame with curving lines, decorative but not overly ornate, covered in a bold floral quilt with matching pillows. Around the windows hung a more subdued fabric, displaying the same pattern in a smaller print. A few watercolor landscapes brightened the pale yellow walls. A bedside table supported a fresh bouquet that nearly matched the bedspread. Under her feet, a blue-and-white rug lay over carefully preserved hardwood. All of it managed to look perfectly haphazard and totally put together at the same time.

She could never live here.

Turning once more, she noticed something laid out on the bed—

"What is that?" Allie pointed accusingly at the nightie. It was cotton eyelet with embroidered pastel roses. Very sheer. Very short. Very low-cut.

"Our housekeeper prepared the room for you. You're welcome to wear it if you want, otherwise, just hang it up and forget about it."

She met Erik's guileless eyes, unamused. "Thanks. I brought my own."

"Okay." His smile didn't waver. "Anything else you need tonight?"

No. "Not a thing, thanks."

"Good night then." He grasped her shoulders and pressed a kiss to her forehead, standing just far enough away that she didn't feel she needed to call him on it. "Welcome to Morningside, Allie. I'm really glad you decided to come. We'll have a great time."

"I'm sure we will."

Another kiss, this one on her cheek, and a closer embrace, just this side of platonic. She had to admit he smelled good, expensive and masculine, but that was about it for her attraction. After he left, she hurried to close the door.

Fifteen minutes later, Allie had unpacked and was lying in bed, listening to Erik humming through the connecting door—locked, she'd checked—and the faint lap of waves outside, nothing at all like the honk-and-siren sounds of Manhattan. The earplugs she wore every night still lay on her bedside table, waiting for her to get sleepy enough to put them in. As long as she was wideawake, she might as well tune in to the natural world around her.

An hour later, she was still lying there. The swishing of the waves had gotten more vigorous and the wind had picked up. She could hear Erik snoring.

It had been a while since Allie had tried to sleep in a new bed—alone, anyway. Apparently she was bad at it. And this room made her feel as though she had to be sure she didn't drool or sweat during the night. Her someday-mansion would feel welcoming and comfortable to anyone. Even her brothers.

She put the earplugs in, hoping they'd trigger some kind of Pavlovian sleep response.

They didn't.

Finally the obvious hit her.

No one was forcing her to lie here. Erik was asleep; no one else was around. She'd wanted to go for a moonlit walk? She could do that. Right now. Sliding out of bed, she stuffed the earplugs into the pocket of her sleep shirt.

Hell, if she wanted to, she could dance naked on the beach all night long.

CHAPTER THREE

JONAS TURNED ONTO I-87 from Route 7, after skirting Albany. Forty-five minutes, give or take, and he'd be at Morningside a day earlier than expected. Funny, now that he was on his way, he couldn't get there fast enough. The feel of the breeze, the way the woods smelled, the sand under his feet, the clear water around his body—it was like returning to the best part of his childhood. Maybe it was the best part. The one place his parents had relaxed their rules, or at least some of them.

His client had canceled dinner that afternoon, then Sandra texted him that she'd agreed to take over a Friday night gig for an ill friend, so would be delayed leaving. She'd encouraged him to go without her, saying she'd drive out the next morning. Jonas had protested, but not very strenuously—the idea of leaving the hot, crowded city behind him after a long week had been too seductive.

And Allie. What was it about a few perfunctory emails that had intrigued him so much? He knew plenty of smart, funny women in Boston. Most likely his memory of her from that dinner at Christmastime had been warped by time into a fantasy. Fantasy had an unfortunate way of beating reality. Case in point: he had believed Missy was a good life-match for him, while she'd been off spending his money and screwing one of her investment firm colleagues.

Plus, Erik might truly like Allie in a deeper way than usual, and she might have changed and truly like him. Someone like Allie would be good for Erik, settle him down, give him something to think and care about other than his own needs and desires.

Blink 182's *Neighborhoods* ended; he fumbled around for his iPod and selected his favorite Red Hot Chili Peppers album, *Stadium Arcadium*, absently wondering what kind of music Allie liked, and whether Erik had entertained or appalled her on the drive up with his penchant for hard rock and heavy metal.

He'd better get Allie out of his head. Erik had described this trip as his best chance with the woman he wanted to marry. Jonas wouldn't break the brother code of ethics by trying to get close to her himself.

But he might have to come to terms someday with being hot for his sister-in-law.

ALLIE STOOD AT the lake's edge, enjoying the water's surprising warmth lapping at her feet. This was fabulous! The moon was just over half full, but so bright, even through a thin layer of cloud cover, that she hadn't bothered bringing out her flashlight. The pleasantly cool breeze kept any bugs at bay. She'd made a good decision to come out here instead of lying in that too-perfect room trying to force her body to sleep.

She strolled toward the boathouse, relishing the rolling splash of waves, the distant creak of tree trunks, the occasional glimpse of a bat. At the boathouse, she peered inside a window and was able to discern a few shadows that might be canoes or kayaks, she wasn't sure.

Farther up the beach and toward the woods, the cottage tempted her. Moving closer, she could see a deck on the beach side of the house, on which sat a table and chairs. The perfect spot for sunning, reading or sipping cocktails. At the door, she hesitated before trying the knob. Locked up tight, she was sure.

It wasn't.

Feeling guilty for preempting Erik's tour, she couldn't resist her curiosity and pushed the door open. The cottage was dimly lit by the moonlight through the windows, but she could make out a cozy cabin with all the comforts of home—even what appeared to be a tiny kitchen. This was her kind of luxury.

Feeling the need to be quiet, even though there was no way Erik could hear her, she tiptoed around the couch, past the fireplace, toward stairs to what turned out to be a charming bedroom with a wall of windows facing the lake. She crossed to the bed, a king on a frame high enough that sleepers could easily see the view, climbed on it and shuffled on her knees toward the glass to look out at the water. Somewhere close by, a loon called out, a long, mournful cry and trill. What a wonderful place to sleep, tucked away almost in the woods, yet close to the lake. If this were her property, she wouldn't go near the big house.

Erik wouldn't even have to know if she slept there tonight. She'd wake up early with the sun most likely, and be back in the main house before he stirred. Judging by how often he was late to work in the mornings, he was not an early riser.

She pulled back the covers to find soft cotton sheets waiting for her. The pillows were piled high, real down pillows like those at Dad's, the kind her family hadn't been able to afford. They always had enough to eat—that was their luxury.

Temptation warred inside her with a touch of anxiety. This wasn't her home. Erik had his mother's room prepared for her. There might be some reason she shouldn't be out here. Maybe Jonas would want to stay in the cottage when he arrived the next day.

Or it might be completely fine.

Unable to decide, she cheated by lying down on top of the bed, scooting to the side closest to the windows. Within minutes she was yawning, as if it were completely natural to her body to sleep there. Giving in with only a slight qualm, she fished out her earplugs, put them in and let herself drift off.

JONAS INCHED HIS Toyota Camry to a halt a few yards from his brother's beloved Mercedes sports coupe. The wind had picked up considerably in the last half hour, so there was little chance Erik or Allie would hear him arrive. He cut the engine, got out and inhaled the gusting lake air greedily. It was nice to be back. Assuming the place sold quickly, this would probably be his last pleasure trip here. Visits from now on would involve packing, sorting, throwing stuff away...

He didn't want to think about that now.

Lifting his bag out of the backseat, he closed the door and walked up to the dark, still house, where Erik and Allie were sleeping. Alone? Together? Alone tonight at least, he decided. Erik would wait until Allie was comfortable here before he made the big move.

For a full minute, Jonas stood in the clearing, gazing at Morningside. Again, he was gripped by emotions—longing, pleasure, affection. Many years of good times in that house, going back as far as his recollections.

A burst of wind brought the first drops of rain and he turned toward the cottage, which Clarissa, the wife of their caretaker, George, kept cleaned, aired out and well-stocked, as well as the house. He'd texted Erik that he'd be arriving a day early but wasn't sure his brother had read the message, since he hadn't replied. Barging into the house unexpectedly could be an unpleasant surprise. Jonas didn't want his second meeting with Allie to take place in the middle of the night after he'd just terrified her. And he wasn't in the mood to face his brother's smug I'm-gonna-score-this-weekend certainty.

A grumble of thunder quickened his steps across the neatly mown grass that managed to grow in the sandy soil by the house. He stepped into the cottage just as the storm hit, wiped a drop of rain off his forehead and grinned at the familiar, dimly lit interior. This had been his refuge when he was too teenager-cool for his old room and his parents.

He spent a few minutes walking around, touching old memories. Still-life paintings his grandmother Bridget had done of flower gardens and seashell-strewn beaches. Knickknacks bought on various family trips abroad—his mother's clan had been avid travelers. Fertility figures from Ghana, nesting dolls from Russia, stone turtles from Hawaii…

Wind and rain buffeted the house, making creaks that sounded like soft footsteps overhead. Jonas unpacked his toiletry kit, brushed his teeth and washed his face in the kitchen sink. The upstairs, with no windows facing west, would be black as a cave, and he'd forgotten to bring a flashlight. The little cottage had never been wired for electric power.

Lightning illuminated the stairs as he made his way toward them. He loved lying in bed watching storms like this blow over the water.

In the bedroom, he dumped his clothes, found the bed by feel and crawled in naked, enjoying the moonless midnight-blackness between the flashes of lightning, already growing further apart.

It was a fast-moving storm, probably not that close. He wouldn't see much drama up here tonight. One summer a house across the lake had been badly damaged by a lightning strike.

Closing his eyes, he relaxed, concentrating on the steady pummeling of rain on the roof, directly over his head. He'd had good times in this bed. Lost his virginity here, when their summer neighbor Sally Sampson, older than he was by a few years, decided it was time he got started.

He hadn't objected.

She'd sneaked into the cottage one night and had woken him with her mouth, doing things that at that age he'd only read about....

Nice memory. His dick certainly remembered, was already standing hopefully at attention. Jonas shifted to his side, experiencing a mild disorientation when the king mattress seemed to move too much.

What was that?

Probably sinus pressure messing with his sense of balance and motion. Long drives could bring it on. Storms usually made it worse.

The cottage hadn't seen any action from him since Sally. The first and only time he'd invited a girlfriend up here, his parents had gone so ridiculously overboard making sure they were never alone long enough to have sex, that Maria had gone home days early and dumped him soon after. He hadn't bothered trying again. His parents firmly believed that all women wanted from Erik and Jonas was to get pregnant and trap them and their Meyer money. Given his experience with Missy, he was starting to wonder if they were onto something.

His eyes opened. Allie wasn't in that camp if she'd resisted Erik for this long.

Lightning flashed.

Huh? In his peripheral vision, he could have sworn...

It flashed again.

What the—

Allie?

Good God. Had he conjured her up? Hallucinated her? Why

didn't he notice her before when lightning lit the room? Did she know he was there?

He stared at the blackness, frozen in surprise, heart pounding. What now?

Maybe she didn't know he was there. Maybe she'd been in the bathroom when he came upstairs? Crazy coincidence.

"Allie," he called softly.

No answer.

The storm renewed itself, rain that had been tapering off hammered again, thunder rumbled louder.

Back asleep already? She couldn't be. Sleepwalking, then?

"Allie?" He tried louder, worried he'd terrify her. His heart had nearly stopped when he saw her, but at least he knew she and Erik were on the property. She thought he was still in Boston.

Maybe he should just sneak out. If she caught him, okay, at least he'd be an intruder in her bedroom, not in her bed.

Small problem: he was naked. Should he get out of the bed and risk fumbling for his clothes on the floor? Better just to go downstairs and get more from his bag.

Another problem: she'd been able to get into bed with him, and he'd registered her only peripherally, but he was considerably larger. If he moved, she'd notice.

Damn.

A bad situation. He'd just have to choose one of the equally bad options.

As carefully as he could, Jonas lifted the covers…

ALLIE'S EYES SHOT open in the dark. What the *hell* was that? The mattress had moved. She swore it had.

It moved again.

Erik.

She was going to kill him.

No, torture him, and then kill him.

Of all the sleazy….

She tore out her earplugs, unaware the storm had gotten so bad. Why hadn't she brought a flashlight?

Lightning provided what she needed: a view of Erik, in bed next to her! The jerk!

She didn't think twice, turned and shoved him with her feet as hard as she could. He shot off the bed and landed with a thud on the floor.

"Ow!"

Served him right. "What the hell do you think you're trying to pull?"

"Nothing!"

"For God's sake, Erik," she shouted. Honestly. The only thing stupider than a horny guy was…an amoeba.

"I'm not Erik," he bellowed. A flash of lightning showed that he'd stood up. He wasn't wearing anything. And he wasn't Erik.

Jeez-o-Pete. The Meyer slimeball brothers. What had Jonas thought? A few friendly emails meant he could just sneak into her bedroom and—

She blinked, her brain catching up to her eyeballs. *What* a great body.

"What are you doing here? You're not even supposed to be here. Especially not *naked!*"

The rain slacked off abruptly, leaving her last word shrieked into relative silence.

"Allie." Lightning showed him holding the bedspread over his best bits. "I didn't know you were in here. I came to the cottage so I wouldn't bother you and Erik, arriving at the big house so late."

Her breath was still coming fast. She didn't know when she'd experienced such a huge adrenaline rush, first fear, then anger. So it took a while for his words to sink in. To process them. To make them appear possible. The rain calmed further.

"Just hang on. Let me get dressed and find a light."

She waited, trying to understand what had happened. She'd been asleep. Had woken up, needing to use the bathroom. Had trouble finding it, trouble using it in the total darkness. Made her way carefully back, annoyed at the lightning for holding off when she needed its brilliance. She'd gotten back into bed and sensed him when he moved.

She heard a thud, followed by a curse. Allie grinned savagely in the dark, still shaky and breathless. Served him right. "Having fun?"

"Oh, yeah. Thanks. I'm sure I can just hobble for the rest of my life. Hold on, there's a kerosene lamp over here somewhere."

Long pause. Another thud. Another curse. Allie snorted. This sounded like a Three Stooges movie.

"You don't *have* to enjoy my pain."

"Oh, yes, I do."

"There." A glimmer as he struck a match, then fed the flame to the wick of a kerosene lamp and replaced the chimney. A soft glow filled the room and showed that he was now wearing jeans. And that he was even more gorgeous than she remembered, with Erik's blue eyes and strong chin, but darker hair, thicker and curling.

No, no. Until he proved he didn't deserve her fury and outrage, she could not risk melting into lust.

"So." She crossed her arms over her chest, wishing he wasn't getting his second view of her with advanced bedhead and no makeup, wearing a shapeless sleep shirt. "What happened?"

"My dinner appointment tonight canceled, I texted Erik that I was coming. I arrived, came up here, got into bed and you joined me." He lifted his hands and let them slap down on his thighs. Long, solid, very nice thighs. Not that she was looking. "Nice to see you again, by the way."

"Well…oh." What was she supposed to do with that story? So devoid of evil or plot or menace of any kind. Almost disappointing.

"I'm sorry I scared you, Allie. If it's any consolation, I nearly had a heart attack when I saw you next to me. I thought I was alone in here, had started drifting off, listening to the rain, then the lightning flashed and guess what?" He mimed comic terror, clutching his chest, mouth hanging open, eyes bulging with shock.

Allie smiled unwillingly and shrugged, her breathing slowing down. "Well, I guess it's just a big, weird mess."

"I guess." He was standing by the bed watching her, hands on his hips, jeans slung low, chest bare. She hugged herself more tightly, hoping she was covering her nipples adequately because they were reaching for him like baby birds for Mama.

The silence stretched. She had a sudden fantasy of him lunging for her, dragging her down on the bed and covering her mouth with his, her breasts with his hands, her—

"You want a beer or something?"

"Yes." Her breath rushed out in relief. "I would love a beer or something."

"Clarissa usually leaves some in the fridge downstairs. Let's check it out."

Carrying the kerosene lamp, he led the way downstairs, accompanied by a distant growl of thunder and the now-gentle patter of rain.

There was indeed beer in the refrigerator, plenty of it, plus wine, champagne, at least two kinds of cheeses, orange juice, limes and tonic. The cottage was clearly party central. Jonas opened two bottles of Bass Ale and offered Allie a glass, which she declined.

They sat at the small pale yellow table in the kitchen area with the lamp between them spreading its light surprisingly far into the room.

"Why isn't there power in the cottage?" Allie took a sip of her beer. She generally preferred a lighter brew, but right now the Bass was seriously working for her. Probably the circumstances. Undoubtedly the man. "Wait, and if there's no electricity, how is there a refrigerator?"

"It runs on gas, like the stove and water heater. My great-grandfather wired the big house for electricity but was stubborn on keeping this place 'pure.' Grandma Bridget felt the same way when she inherited it, and it just stayed that way. I like it."

"I do, too. It's sort of romantic."

He chose that moment to put down his beer and meet her eyes. "It is."

Allie had trouble breathing. What was it about him? The dim light, the smooth gold of his skin out of which his blue eyes blazed, the fact that he was incredibly handsome and hot and she'd just seen him naked? Yeah, that might be it.

Ulp. She needed to break the silence, but her mind had gone blank. She could only sit there gawking stupidly at him.

"So, are we okay with everything?"

"Oh." Allie brought herself out of her daze. "Well, sort of."

"I know." He shook his head, looking perplexed. "I'm not straight on some of it, either. Where were you before you got into bed with me?"

"Bathroom. Why didn't you say something?"

"I didn't know you were there until the lightning showed you."

She narrowed her eyes skeptically over her beer, which was already half-gone. "I climbed into *bed* with you, and you didn't notice?"

"It was dark. The proverbial couldn't-see-my-hand-in-front-of-my-face dark."

"The mattress must have bounced."

"I felt nothing." He gestured toward her, up and down. "You're a wee thing."

Allie snorted. "Come on."

"Okay." Jonas pushed back his chair and stood. He narrowed his eyes, which made him look bad-boy fierce and even sexier. "You don't believe me? Come on. We'll reenact it."

"No, no…"

"Look, my honor is on the line here." He picked up the lamp and headed for the stairs.

Allie hesitated a moment, then left with the choice of being abandoned in a dark, unfamiliar room versus being upstairs in a bedroom with a god among men, she followed him.

She was not stupid.

"Lie down." He set the lamp on the bedside table and pointed to the bed. "Here, where I was."

"Fine." Allie lay on the edge of the mattress.

"Now close your eyes. I'll lie on the other side. Bear in mind I've got at least sixty pounds on you."

"Okay." She closed her eyes and waited. When he climbed on, the mattress tugged and dipped some, but nothing like the earthquake she'd expected.

"Anything?"

"Yes. But, okay, not that much."

"If I was as light as you, and you were changing position at the same time, you might not feel anything."

"Hmm." She kept her eyes closed. "I *guess* I might not."

"Come on, victory is mine. Admit it."

She turned her head to scoff, trying not to let on that she was pretty fired up being this close to him. "I admit nothing."

"Coward."

"Okay, okay." She held up her hands. "It's plausible. I'll give you that much."

"I even said your name. Twice."

"Oh." Allie pointed to both sides of her head. "Earplugs."

"Ah. That explains that. I thought about tapping you on the shoulder but I was afraid I'd give you a coronary."

"You probably would have."

"Good thing I didn't." He stretched out his arms, folded them behind his head and settled himself comfortably, closing his eyes. "So with that cleared up, you want to go to sleep?"

"What?"

"Why not?" He peeked at her, and then closed his eyes again, smiling faintly. "I like being in bed with you."

Allie struggled up on her elbows, squinting down at him, grinning in spite of herself. "Oh, really."

"Yeah. I mean it's a little weird, since we don't know each other, but look, we've got it all here. Excitement, drama, intrigue, possible conspiracy." He turned to look up at her, stubble darkening his jaw and highlighting his cheekbones. "Everything."

Allie's smile faded. She swallowed awkwardly. Those eyes were dragging her into him. The attraction was so powerful she could barely maintain the contact. Her gaze flicked to his mouth before she could stop herself. A beautiful mouth, masculine and full. She'd like to—

"I was kidding. I'll walk you back to the house."

"Oh." She jerked her gaze back to his. "Yes, sure. Thanks."

He didn't move, didn't look away. "Okay, mostly kidding."

Allie drew in a breath, face and body heating. "I see."

"I can't, though. Erik."

Allie shook her head quickly. "I have no romantic feelings for Erik."

"None?" His intense gaze got more intense. She had a crazy feeling he was pleased. Was that ego or real interest? Erik talked about Jonas as if he were a straight arrow, not a player by any means.

"No. He's a great guy. But not for me."

"He has feelings for you."

She wanted to laugh. "He *thinks* he does."

"Maybe. But he's my brother." Jonas sat up, clutched his chest and gazed off into the distance with comic gravity. "Therefore we must venture out. Together…but alone."

Allie giggled. Erik hadn't mentioned his brother had a playful side. "Yes, my liege. Through storm and peril we shall uh, whatever."

"Yeah, that." He came around the bed and gave her a hand up. She came face-to-face with him, nearly chest-to-chest. Well, her face to his neck, her chest to his upper abdomen. He was tall. Probably six-two. She was barely five-four.

"I look forward to getting to know you, Allie." He smiled warmly, a touch of mischief in his blue eyes that brought out more of his resemblance to his carefree brother. "Too bad we'll have to leave it at that."

CHAPTER FOUR

"JONAS SAID, 'TURN RIGHT on driveway after the big blue mailbox.' Okay." Sandra scanned the side of the road, her wipers going full power. Blue? She couldn't tell blue from orange in the dark, and the rain wasn't helping. Wait…there was a mailbox. Big, yes. Blue? She had no idea, but she was turning. Who would build a house out here in the middle of east bejeezus on purpose? Besides Bigfoot? She'd bet there wasn't a decent slice of pizza or cup of coffee within fifty miles. Forget mani-pedis.

Her tires bumped and bounced, sending her swaying back and forth. Secondhand car—its suspension was already shot when she bought it five years earlier. Ahead of her, the road continued through the rain-blurred woods as far as her headlights reached. Lord have mercy, Jonas called this a driveway? No. Driveways were about fifty feet long with nice, smooth pavement.

She should have waited to drive up until the next morning, but she hated mornings. Getting up any time before ten required an entire pot of coffee. And when Gina, the "sick" friend Sandra had agreed to cover for tonight—she glanced at the car's clock—make that *last* night, had made up with her boyfriend, she'd also miraculously recovered from her illness and could perform. Which meant Sandra was able to come early and surprise Jonas.

Lightning illuminated a clearing ahead. Thank you, God. Must be the place. Two cars were there already: the insatiable Erik's and that of the very enticing and wonderful Jonas Meyer.

She didn't entirely regret ending their sexual relationship— how many years ago now? Eight? Well, okay, sometimes she did regret it. He was hot and she was human. But it had been the right thing to do. She'd started having more than casual feelings for Jonas, had started seeing him as an easy rescue from her financial and personal struggles. The problem with that? Jonas hadn't given up on true love yet, and as much as he adored her, she knew she was never going to be "the one."

Three years after she cut off their contact, they'd bumped into each other and met up shortly afterward for such a nice lunch that they'd decided to stay in touch. He was probably one of her closest friends.

Ever since Jonas's nasty breakup with that bitch Missy left him cynical and bruised, Sandra had been wondering if hooking up together permanently could still work out. They enjoyed each other. The sex had been great. They both liked kids. And, oh yes, his lovely money would make her life a hell of a lot easier. She was thirty-four and had just about reached the end of her tolerance for a life lived paycheck to paycheck. Not to mention she had next to nothing saved for retirement.

They'd joked about ending up together, but she had a feeling neither of them had been totally joking. Maybe this was the weekend to have a serious talk with him if the opportunity presented itself.

As she brought the car to a stop, the rain let up and visibility improved enough that she could see around her. Nice lake. Cute little cabin on the beach. Farther in, by the edge of the woods, the house. No, that couldn't be it. Too small. There it was, nearly behind her. A mega-mansion, all lit up as if it was some kind of monument.

She took a moment to breathe and tamp down the pain inside her. *Ancient history, honey.* This life didn't belong to her anymore, hadn't since she left home and then her marriage. She had no one to blame but herself for losing it all, and no one but herself to rely on if she wanted it back now. Living hand-to-mouth had been a satisfying rebellion in her twenties, but not so much in her thirties. Afterward came the forties and fifties, when her appeal to men her own age would wane. God knew she wasn't going to get rich performing, and she didn't have the brains or patience to go back to school. If she wanted financial security, she'd have to start nailing him down now.

Practical, yes, but a bit sickening. She certainly hadn't expected to end up in this situation when she'd marched defiantly out of her parents' lives. Ah, the stupidity of pampered youth.

Apparently she'd expected that money would just keep showing up, as it always had.

The rain started coming down harder again. She cut the engine, grabbed her overnight bag from the passenger seat and bolted for the mega-mansion's front door before it decided to pour again. Peering up, she couldn't see any lights on in the house, not that she expected to. Most people were asleep at this hour. Performers were a different breed.

Not wanting to wake anyone, she tried the door, even though she was sure it would be locked against the inevitable psycho with a shotgun who favored remote lake areas.

The door wasn't locked.

Sweet Jesus, these Meyers were certifiable.

Making her way inside the house, she shut the storm out behind her, locking the door as any sensible person would, and found a switch that bathed the entry in warm light. Wow. Look at this chilly museum of a place. She tried to picture Jonas as a kid, probably not allowed to bring sand or candy inside. Feeling as if you weren't welcome or didn't belong in your own home sucked. She should know.

No wonder he leaned toward the conservative side. A place like this would beat the wildness out of anyone. It was a beach house, for heaven's sake. Even her uptight parents decorated their place in the Hamptons with summery stuff. Nautical print rugs, painted buoys and model ships, seashell upholstery on the furniture, paintings of oceanscapes and sailboats on the walls. No big shock that Jonas wanted to sell. This wasn't a house you fell in love with. He'd mentioned buying a place on Cape Cod. She could seriously get behind that concept.

Climbing the stairs, she heard a door open and saw a man stumble out into the hallway. Not Jonas. Erik, then. Drunk? Or sleepy?

"Hello?" She reached the landing in time to see him turn toward her voice.

Well. Jonas's brother was adorable. Not that she was surprised, given his success with women. Kind of a more casual, blonder version of Jonas, carrying a few more pounds that softened him and made him seem more approachable. The kind of guy you'd slap on the back instead of shake hands with.

"I'm Sandra McKinley."

"Sandra." He blinked his baby blues in confusion. "I thought you were coming tomorrow."

She spread her hands to say whatcha-gonna-do, adopting the South Boston persona she'd created for herself so long ago that it was nearly instinctive. "Tomorrow is today now. And I'm here."

"What time is it?"

"Two a.m. Where's Jonas?"

"Not coming until tomorrow. I mean today."

"No, baby, he's here now."

"Hmm." His eyes focused on her, his mouth twisted in a half grin. Cute. Definitely cute. A very boyish thirty. *"Baby?"*

"You don't like it?" She shrugged. "I'll call you something else."

"Erik works." He put his hands on his hips, looking swagger-confident in an old T-shirt and boxers. "I remember now, Jonas texted me about showing up early."

"Uh-huh. Where does he sleep? East wing? West wing? North? South? How many wings you got in this place?"

He laughed easily. "The house too much for you, *baby?*"

"Not for me." She folded her arms across her chest. "Nothing's too much for me."

"Well, well." He took a step closer and pointed down the hall, fully alert now. Not drunk then, just groggy. "Jonas usually sleeps in the last room there on the right. I'm sure he'd love you to join him. If you want your own room, there's one made up for you across the hall."

She was only mildly surprised that he thought they were still lovers. Erik and Jonas weren't the closest of brothers. And Jonas wasn't big on sharing personal information.

"Thanks. Anything else I need to know?"

"Bathroom's behind me on the left. No, your right. Towels are in the closet opposite if there aren't any in your room." He jerked his thumb over his shoulder, not taking his eyes off her. "Should be a robe in your room, too."

Sandra stared back, expecting him to drop his gaze. He didn't. "What's the matter, you never seen a woman before?"

"Thousands." He didn't look remotely apologetic. "But Jonas didn't tell me."

"Didn't tell you what?" She let her arms drop to her sides, sure she'd just handed him the opportunity for one of his favorite lines.

Here it came.

"That you were so beautiful. So exotic, like Salma Hayek. And so…" He gestured toward her body. "Beautiful."

"Ah, I see." She pretended complete nonchalance, but deep down she was pleased even knowing his reputation as a flatterer. "Should he have told you?"

"Maybe not." Erik shrugged. "Most men would brag."

"Jonas isn't most men."

Erik rolled his eyes. "So I keep hearing."

Ah, sibling envy. Interesting, since Erik wasn't exactly passed over when it came to handing out gifts. He had the looks and charm and was good at his job, too, from what Jonas had told her, as well as being a connoisseur of food and wine. But family dynamics didn't thrive on logic. They often thrived in spite of it.

"It's very nice to meet you, Erik. I look forward to getting to know you better this weekend." She gave him a sultry smile because why not, and started down the hall, rolling her suitcase along, swinging her hips since she was sure he was watching.

"Oh, Sandra. Jonas might not be up here. Sometimes he sleeps in the cottage."

"Cottage?" Sandra turned, smirking. "You mean that whole other *house* outside?"

He smirked back. "You got a problem with money, Sandra?"

"Only in that I don't have enough, Erik."

He chuckled, a laugh remarkably similar to his brother's. "I like you. You're not Jonas's type at all."

"No? Whose type am I?" When he just kept grinning, she and her suitcase turned back and started again down the hall. "See you in the morning, baby. Butler serving breakfast?"

"Yuh-huh. Seven a.m. sharp. You miss it, you don't eat."

"I'll see what I can manage to—"

A frantic pounding came at the front door, then the sound of male laughter and a female squeal, followed by a cascade of giggles.

Sandra turned to stare at Erik, who stared back. "Expecting company?"

"It sounds like—"

The front door burst open.

"We made it." Jonas's voice, out of breath. "Thank God I remembered the extra key."

"I'm soaked!" Unidentified woman's voice.

Behind Sandra, Erik's footsteps, approaching fast. Apparently that unidentified voice was now identified.

Sandra descended the curve of the staircase with Erik close behind. And there they were, Jonas and Allie, dripping wet, smiling at each other in a way that people who had only just met generally didn't, and standing much closer than strangers usually did, even if they were very nearsighted. Which Jonas, at least, wasn't.

Sandra's heart contracted sharply. Jealousy, unwelcome and unwarranted. Allie was supposed to be Erik's project up here. Jonas was supposed to be hers.

Above them, on the landing, her suitcase fell over with a loud thud.

Jonas and Allie looked up.

There was a brief and deliciously awkward silence.

"Sandra," Jonas said cheerfully.

"Hello, Jonas," she replied calmly.

"Allie!" Erik, mildly apoplectic.

"Oh. Hi, Erik." Allie spoke too loudly, her tone a combination of guilty and giddy.

Well.

What an *int*eresting weekend they were all going to have.

Text from Allie: Julie, you would not believe what happened tonight. It involves Jonas, me and a bed. Nothing actually happened, but it felt like it could have. People magazine knows nothing. This is the sexiest man alive.

ALLIE'S EYES FLEW OPEN. Morning. How early was it? She squinted
at her watch. Nearly eight. She hadn't slept well, not surprising
after all the excitement the night before. Terror and titillation
and tremendous awkwardness. She and Jonas had run out of the
cottage, intending to head straight for the main house, but Jonas
had grabbed her hand and swerved, leading them down to the
lake. The rain really let them have it then, but instead of escap-
ing, they'd sprinted, splashing, along the water's edge, getting
soaked and having a total, exhilarating, childish blast. Allie was
a sucker for men who could play. After meeting Jonas in New
York, as polished and interesting as he was, she wouldn't have
thought he had that in him.

Yum.

Back inside, breathless and laughing, they'd found Erik and
Sandra sending them such icy looks she was surprised the water
hadn't frozen on their bodies.

A waste of their energy. Jonas and Allie's fun had been entirely innocent.

Well, mostly innocent.

Okay, buried under a thick layer of sexual tension there had
probably been a speck of innocence somewhere.

Sigh.

With the four of them there, together for the first time, it had
been hard to know what to say to whom, how to frame their entrance, or whether to apologize for something they hadn't really
done. It was a complicated mess, with relationships among the
quartet poorly defined all the way around. Were Jonas and Sandra really just friends? Had Erik really told his brother he had
feelings for Allie? Did he?

Allie had no idea. The best thing to do was get up, have breakfast and start over. But first, she'd scramble out of bed and have
a long look out the window—being careful not to leave smudges
or fingerprints or shed skin cells on anything.

The morning was glorious. A cool breeze blew in through the
screen and the lake sparkled in the sun, shining out of a cloud-
less sky. Ahhh, much better than the city, at least for this week.

She showered and dressed in black shorts with a peacock

feather design—from the Artists & Fleas market in Brooklyn, her favorite source for relatively inexpensive secondhand clothing—and a simple white top. Minimal makeup. She wasn't out to seduce anyone. Right, Sandra? Right, Erik?

At least she probably wasn't.

Ready for the day, she wandered out into the hall, noting the still-closed doors. Nobody up but her? Erik had said breakfast was a free-for-all, that their house elf, Clarissa, would have stocked the kitchen and they could rummage around and grab whatever they wanted.

She was fine with that. In fact, it would be good to grab a bite and have a leisurely jolt of caffeine to fortify herself before she had to deal with anyone else.

Except…Jonas was already up, standing with his back to her, barefoot in the cinnamon-smelling, sparkling clean, nearly antiseptic kitchen. He was wearing a royal-blue T-shirt that emphasized the breadth of his shoulders and khaki cargo shorts that emphasized the sexy shape of his ass.

"Good morning."

"Hey, Allie, good morning." He swung around, wearing a natural grin that made her relax. There might be lingering tension with Sandra and Erik this morning, but at least she had an ally. "How did you sleep?"

She debated whether to be polite or honest, and chose the middle ground. "Not too bad."

"But not too good? Same here. Coffee?" He pointed to the pot. "I'll pour."

"Love some." She perched on a stool by the huge kitchen island, thinking how much more welcoming and cute the cottage kitchen was than this stainless steel, white-countered bastion of state-of-the-art perfection. She would have loved to see the kitchen original to the house.

"Clarissa's got fresh fruit for us and pecan cinnamon rolls. That sound okay?"

"I thought I smelled heaven. That sounds wonderful." She accepted her mug and sipped gratefully. The brew was dark, rich and strong, just the way she liked it.

"I'm guessing Erik and Sandra will be asleep for a while." Jonas pulled a pan of the fragrant rolls out of the oven. "They're both night owls and late sleepers. So we're on our own for a few more hours."

"Okay." She liked the sound of that, but not the concept of him being familiar with Sandra's sleeping habits.

"I was wondering if you wanted to go kayaking on the lake."

"Sure, I would love that." Allie twisted her lips wryly. "At least I think I would."

"You've never been in a kayak?" He asked offhandedly—not as if he'd never heard of anything so outrageous—and set out a plate and napkin for each of them.

"Nope." Her family's idea of summer water sports was to fight the crowds at public pools in Brooklyn, a fact she'd stopped admitting after her friend Melanie made a huge deal about how disgusting they were.

"I think you'll enjoy it."

She hoped so. And that she wouldn't be completely inept. The women Jonas knew were probably all kayak experts. Sandra was likely a national kayak champion, though she didn't look the sporty type. She seemed to be more of a city girl, like Allie, only more beautiful, more voluptuous, more exotic, probably more experienced in bed...

Ugh. She was tying herself up in knots. Julie accused her of overthinking everything, especially where men were concerned. Julie was undoubtedly right. Allie would do her best to think of Jonas's interest in her as a different version of his brother's knee-jerk flirtation, nothing to do with his feelings for her, personally. Because the more she fantasized them into a relationship the more it would hurt when he dragged Sandra into his bedroom tonight. The fact that he could turn Allie on by biting into a cinnamon roll would remain her little secret.

The fact that *she* could get turned on by biting into a cinnamon roll wouldn't. "Oh my heaven, these are amazing. Does Clarissa make them?"

"She gets them from a bakery in town." Jonas sat opposite her at the kitchen island. "They'll have to build a cardiac hospital in Lake George if people keep eating them."

"Worth it." She licked buttery frosting off her lips. "A shorter life is a small price to pay."

"You know I suggested kayaking without thinking." He helped himself to a second roll. "Would you rather get started on the clothes in the attic?"

"Oh, no, there's time for that." Jonas was probably the only thing in the world more tempting to her than the contents of that attic. "Kayaking sounds fun. And I think Erik wanted to show me around…"

"Ah. Right." He nodded abruptly and concentrated on his roll. "Absolutely."

Allie put down her coffee. This warranted a discussion. "Do we have to get weird and tiptoe over who has rights to whom all weekend? I really don't want to."

"No, you're right. We'll keep it simple. You're here with Erik. I'm here with Sandra."

"Okay." Served her right for bringing it up.

"But when they're still asleep…" A slow smile spread over Jonas's face. "We can cheat on them."

Allie giggled, wilting into relief. "That's exactly what I meant!"

"Don't worry." He finished his coffee and took his plate to the sink. "It's not going to be a big deal. Sandra and I are friends…"

Allie jumped on his hesitation. "With privileges?"

"Not anymore."

"She knows that?"

"Her idea. Years ago." He turned back to Allie, not displaying any sign of discomfort that might indicate he was lying. "Last night was weird, but it won't be that way going forward. Erik will calm down. It's all good. We can hang out on kayaks with our consciences clear."

She wasn't totally convinced. Sandra had looked as if she could cheerfully tear Allie apart with her teeth. "Okay."

"But only because kayaks don't have beds in them."

"Huh." Allie shook her head at him, shame-on-you, and devoured the last of her roll's buttery bliss. Kayaking was exercise, right? She'd burn off the calories of one roll paddling for only… twenty-five or twenty-six hours. And if she came back from this outing with Jonas and found Sandra and Erik upset again, that was it. She would make sure she and Jonas weren't alone again.

The idea made her instantly miserable.

After breakfast, she and Jonas changed into their bathing suits, slathered on their sunscreen and met down at the boathouse where Jonas found water shoes that fit her and selected kayaks and paddles. He gave her a short lesson, which, while she was swinging the paddle around on the beach, made Allie even more certain she was going to be hopeless at this.

She wasn't. A little clumsy at first, she soon got the hang of the stroke and was gliding happily around, amazed at how little strength or energy it took to propel the boat forward. The lake water in daylight was astonishingly clear—green when she peered into its depths and a rich dark blue when she gazed across it. Add the vibrant green of the surrounding forested hills and the white of the gulls skimming the surface looking for fish, and she was hooked, not only on kayaking, but on the area.

"This is so gorgeous! How could you not come here every weekend?"

Jonas looked around, resting his paddle. "That's a good question. I guess I got out of the habit."

"I can't imagine." That was an understatement. Not only couldn't she imagine, she wanted to growl at him. If she had a place like this she'd be out here every possible chance she got. That was something about privileged people that drove her crazy. They didn't really understand and value what they had because they'd never done without. Whoever she ended up with would have to have worked hard for everything he owned.

"No." Jonas resumed paddling. "Out of context, it probably doesn't make sense to anyone on the outside. Partly, it's that my family has made this place its own for so many generations that it came to represent something I only had a tiny piece of and couldn't alter. I've wanted my own place for a while now, in my own style, with my own stuff."

"Kind of like how you only have a piece of your company and want to have your own. So…essentially you're a megalomaniac."

"You do understand!" He grinned, then his gaze shifted behind her and he pointed urgently. "Look."

Allie turned just in time to see a bald eagle flying past only a few yards away, its yellow eyes and curved beak clearly, if briefly, visible.

"Oh my gosh!" She shaded her eyes, watching the majestic bird fly, the great wings flapping gracefully as it made its way up the lake. "I could see it so clearly."

"They're around here every year, but I haven't seen one that close up before. It's always thrilling."

"And you stay away from here." She couldn't stop straining her eyes after the bird, now a distant miniature.

"You'd get it if you saw our family in action. My dad was extremely controlling. Erik and I both rebelled in our own way. He fought back. I tended to disappear. I still feel as if I have to behave myself in the house, even when they're not there."

She thought of him outside last night, splashing around in the rain, and wondered if that little moment of messy exuberance would have been forbidden, too. Her own mom had plenty of rules, but they tended to pop up one day and be forgotten the next. The chaos theory of parenting. "I understand about tough family dynamics. I lose it if I spent much time back home anymore."

"How long since you've been there?"

"Let's see…" She made herself look gravely pensive. "What century is this?"

His laughter traveled easily over the water. "I'm telling you, you crack me up, Allie."

His compliment pleased her ridiculously. "I was home at Christmas. But I had to be. I'd rather meet Mom or my brothers out somewhere."

"Neutral territory. The old habits and roles can be escaped some. Plus there are witnesses if it comes to murder."

"Yes, so useful." She grinned at him. His gaze lit on hers, then drifted over her head back toward his property.

"Being back now, it does feel different." He shrugged. "Too late, since we're selling."

"You have a buyer?"

"No."

"Then it's not too late."

"Mentally too late. I've let go. Erik has, too."

She nodded. Not her business. But she thought they were nuts to let a place like this slip away.

"Ready to turn back?"

"Regretfully, yes."

Jonas maneuvered his kayak so that he pulled up about a foot from hers. His dark curls had been buffeted by the wind into a bedroom-sexy mess. He pulled down his sunglasses and gave her a breath-stealing smile, blue eyes quiet and sincere. "I also like that you challenge me, Allie McDonald."

She tipped her head coyly, heart fluttering. "That's two things you like about me, Jonas Meyer. This is getting serious."

"Is it? Two whole things?" He frowned. "That seems like an awful lot for someone like you. Too many, actually. Maybe I've gone over the edge."

"You think?" Allie trailed her hand dreamily in the clear water, cupped her fingers and unloaded a nice cold spray on him. Before he could react, she dug in her paddle and headed back the way they'd come, giggling like a crazed fiend.

He followed, but where she expected retaliation, she got none. He couldn't be angry over a little water. Maybe he was waiting for his chance. Maybe he used up all his playfulness the night before.

She turned to find him effortlessly keeping up with her. "Okay, okay. Score one for Allie. I deserved that. We're even."

"Yes!" Allie raised her fist triumphantly over her head. He pulled alongside her and they paddled much more slowly back to the beach.

"I'll land first and help you." Jonas slid the kayak up onto the sand, stepped out and pulled his boat farther up.

Help? Allie didn't need help, she was now one of those expert kayaker women Jonas hung out with. She copied what he'd done, grounding her boat and stepping out into the shallow water. Easy, ha!

A wave caught the kayak and pulled, leaving Allie stuck with one leg in the sand, the other in a boat that was rapidly trying to move away.

She was not good at splits.

Just as she'd managed to get her second foot free and balance, he was there, strong arm holding her. Then his other arm came around her and he scooped her off her feet.

Jeez, overkill rescue. She opened her mouth to tell him she was fine, for heaven's sake, when she found herself sailing through the air.

Splash.

"Oh." She staggered to her feet, sputtering. *"Oh,* you are so going to pay for that. 'We're *even,*' he says."

Without thinking, she rushed him as if he were one of her brothers and splashed with skill born of plenty of practice, until he waded in farther to avoid the assault. *Just a little farther, a little farther...*

Perfect. She gathered herself and leaped, catching him off balance.

Splash.

His turn!

He gave a shout and struggled up, sunglasses knocked askew, and lunged for her. Ha! Amateur. She was already out of reach.

"You are good, Allie."

"Five younger brothers."

"Five!" He shook his head admiringly. "Erik did not train me as well as they trained you."

"Are we even *now?*" She held out her hand.

"Even." He took it and shook. "Though I am sooo tempted right now to—"

"Don't you dare."

He held her hand longer than was necessary, gave it a slight tug so she had to step toward him. "I like the tomboy in you, Allie MacDonald. It brings out...well, it's great."

"You're going to give me a swelled head, Jonas Meyer."

"I'll take that chance." He squeezed her hand, and swam back toward the house as if he said that kind of stuff to women every day.

Maybe he did.

But much too quickly, she was starting to want him to say those things only to her.

CHAPTER FIVE

SANDRA EMERGED FROM her bedroom and headed for the stairs, smiling wryly. What kind of interesting new complications would crop up today? How did Erik spend the night? How would he react to Jonas and Allie this morning? Would he graciously bow out of the game or continue fighting for his uninterested lady? Sandra hoped he'd have the sense to do the former. A lot less messy all around. Erik hadn't hung around long after Jonas and Allie burst in, but long enough for Sandra to see his pain. It was tough to feel betrayed by people you loved. She knew what that was like.

At the same time, Erik was denser than lead if he still thought he had a chance with Allie.

As for Sandra, she'd be fine. She was always fine. Life's speed bumps—in her case molded by her own poor choices—might slow her down, but they never stopped her. Jonas wasn't in love with her, would never be in love with her, and she probably never would have been truly in love with him. Darn it. He had it all—looks, money, sex appeal, money, charm, money, intelligence, money... She'd taken care of herself since she left her rebellious mistake of a marriage at age twenty-two, after sticking with it for five miserable years, mostly out of stubborn pride. The subsequent decision to live her life doing what she loved, even if it paid garbage, had been hers and hers alone, and she'd made it understanding the consequences. Unless she managed to marry rich, no cushy retirement in a tropical resort for her.

At the bottom of the stairs, her smile widened. She resisted the urge to rub her hands together and cackle. Who would be up this morning and what would the atmosphere be like in this very promising soap opera? It was ten-thirty. Jonas had most likely been awake for hours already. She didn't know Erik's and Allie's schedules.

A glance into the kitchen showed Erik, alone, surrounded by white and stainless steel that reminded her of her mother's taste.

So cold, so uninviting, in spite of the wonderful cinnamon smell. Her dream kitchen would be all bright colors and cheerful pictures and cartoons on the refrigerator.

She smiled at Erik, slumped over a cup of coffee at the generous kitchen island, hair endearingly mussed. Tsk-tsk, somebody hadn't slept well. "Well, hello, Erik. I see you're a bright-eyed early bird like me."

"Never miss a sunrise." He waved heavily toward the coffeepot on the white counter. "The lifeblood is ready, help yourself. There are cinnamon rolls, too. Clarissa provided them. She's our caretaker's wife."

"Ah, your *caretaker*. Is that like a babysitter?"

He rubbed his eyes as if his head hurt. "Ha ha."

"I know, I know, I'm hilarious." She poured herself coffee, glancing at him now and then, the great Meyer womanizer, not the arrogant jerk she expected, not quite. His type got lucky by being the nonthreatening buddy, the cute little brother. Then when women were lulled into feeling safe, bam, pants around the ankles. "Allie still asleep?"

"God, no. She gets up at dawn like my brother." His grumpy jealousy was painfully obvious. "They're probably starting their second marathon of the morning."

Sandra shuddered comically. "It's a sickness."

"I'm telling you…"

"And what do they get out of it? Great bodies, good health, energy, long life…"

"Exactly." He brought his hand down on the table. "Total waste of time."

Sandra sipped her coffee, which was predictably excellent, pondering her next move. Talk to him about Allie now? Or stick with the small talk? Maybe she could do both. "So what's your plan for today, Erik?"

"I'm going to show Allie around the property."

"Uh…" Sandra gestured toward the cottage and beach. "I'm guessing she's seen most of it."

He gave a grunt of irritation. "Yeah, well, I'll show her the attic. There are trunks of old clothes up there that belonged to my mom's family going back generations. Allie is a designer. I told her she could have them."

"Cool." She sipped more coffee, judging him and the situation, then decided to risk it. "You like this Allie woman, huh?"

"Maybe." He met her eyes, his so much like Jonas's, but without that steady graveness. His looked ready to dance, though at the moment they were tinged with bitterness. "What's it to you?"

"Me?" She leaned forward as if to whisper. "I'm crazed with jealousy."

Erik cracked a smile. "Yeah, get in line."

"I hear there is one."

"Who told you that?"

She lifted an eyebrow. "Guess."

"Got it." He held her gaze this time, his suddenly bold. "I like women."

"Uh-huh." Sandra sipped her coffee, annoyed that his macho act had given her a little thrill of response. She'd seen men playing this role so many times, she should know better. "So why Allie? What's special about her?"

"You want to know because of how I feel or because of the way Jonas was looking at her last night?"

"What do you think?"

"Not sure." He narrowed his eyes. "I haven't figured you out yet."

She snorted. "Good luck with that. Tell me about Allie."

"She's…" He frowned. "Different."

"From?"

"Other women."

"She used to be a man?"

"What?" Erik nearly choked on his coffee. "God, no."

"How do you know?"

He was laughing now, looking much more handsome than when he'd been grumpy. His eyes were back to dancing. "Actually, you're right. I don't."

"So you mean she's different from your usual type."

"Yeah. She's not…" He pushed his hand through his hair, making it rise to new levels of bedhead. "She's got this innocence about her that is really, really sexy."

Oh, for— It was all Sandra could do to keep from making gagging noises. "Ah. You're one of *those* guys."

"What guys?"

She scoffed. "You spend your life screwing every woman you can and then insist on marrying a virgin."

"Huh?" Erik stopped on the way to his next sip of coffee. "I'm not doing that. Am I doing that?"

"Sounds like it to me." His dismay surprised her. Maybe no one had ever held his behavior up to him for a look. "Tell me more."

"She's more than just sweet and sexy, though. She's funny and smart and sophisticated and ambitious. But also down to earth. Different from the girls I grew up with who had everything handed to them."

"Oh, like you didn't?"

He pointed at her accusingly. "That is not the same."

"Because they're women?"

His infectious grin spread. "Because I'm not trying to date myself."

Sandra laughed. She didn't see that coming. "Good one."

"I had this fantasy that things would work out between us this week." He sighed and leaned back in his chair, stretching mournfully. "But now, I don't know. You saw how she and Jonas were looking at each other last night."

"Hard to miss."

"That didn't bother you?"

"For about ten seconds. Then I got over it."

"Just like that?"

"Just like that. Jonas and I are friends, Erik."

"Yeah?" He stared at her curiously, and then got up. "I'm getting more coffee, you want some?"

"No, thanks."

"Jonas knows I want Allie. They might be having fun, but he won't do anything." He filled his cup and brought it back to the table. "He leaves Wednesday. Then Allie and I will be alone. I could still have a chance."

"Right." Poor delusional fool. But then Sandra had been one herself, more than once. Exhibit A: Of course her parents loved her! Though they never showed the slightest sign of it and reacted to her wanting to marry a creepy thirty-year-old at seventeen not by protecting her, but by disinheriting her. Exhibit B: Of course her husband wasn't abusive; he never hit her! Though he turned out to be a domineering, controlling jerk who made her life hell. Exhibit C: She wasn't really addicted to amphetamines; they just helped her get through the day…

Delusionville. Everyone lived there sometimes. Erik would be particularly susceptible as a spoiled and somewhat clueless rich kid who'd never been set straight. God knew Sandra had encountered plenty of them growing up on the gold coast of Connecticut.

She got up and went to the kitchen window to see the property in daylight. Allie and Jonas stood by the lake on the private beach, water streaming off their bodies, faces close, laughing. Sandra smiled in spite of herself. Yeah, she was crazy about Jonas. Crazy enough to want him to look that happy all the time. Happier than he ever looked when he was with her.

She'd seen his dismay last night when he got a peek at his brother's face. She'd heard the stories over the years, how Jonas was always sacrificing himself for family and friends. Look how he'd dropped everything to come here this weekend for Erik's sake. Look how many times he'd come to Sandra's aid with support, with a willing ear, with words of encouragement, and a couple of times with loans she'd paid off as soon as she could.

Jonas and Allie glanced toward the house. Their bodies seemed to collapse in on themselves. Their smiles disappeared. They started pulling the kayaks back into the boathouse.

She was seized with a sudden, absolutely brilliant idea.

Behind her, Erik was still talking, blah-blah-blah, about how Allie would settle him down, give his life purpose, give him what he'd been searching for all his life without realizing it. Not a word about what would be good for Allie. Sandra would bet Erik didn't know her at all beyond his fantasy of what he wanted her to be.

Sandra would step in. Give Erik a new fantasy, and keep him

out of Jonas's way. In the process, she and Erik could get to know each other. Maybe she'd still have a shot at a life of comfort and security. She doubted she'd ever have deep feelings for Erik, but she was too old and too tired and too broke to hold out for true love.

And, if she engineered the next two minutes exactly right, she and Erik could get a little of their own back after Allie and Jonas's giggly intimate entrance last night.

"I don't know, Erik."

He broke off his monologue. "Don't know what?"

"I don't know if Allie is the right woman for you." She strolled toward him, oh so casually, knowing full well what she was doing and how his male pea-brain would react to her. She knew how to play the game as well as he did.

Probably better.

"What do you mean?"

She sank into a chair opposite him, leaning forward, elbows on the island counter, chin in her hands, pushing her breasts forward and together. *Go on, take a look at that.*

He did. What a surprise. One nervous glance, then another, less nervous.

"I mean let's cut the bull, Erik." She lowered her voice to a soft purr and slowed her speech for maximum effect. "I'm a sexual person. I love sex, I love everything about it, every position and every mood."

He shifted in his chair and made an inarticulate noise.

"One thing sexual people can do without fail is spot other sexual people." She held up her fist and extended her index finger toward him. "You."

Erik stopped fidgeting. "Yes."

"In the long term, we can't be happy except with people like ourselves. You know what I mean? You and I, we want it all the time. Any time of day, any time of night. You say the word and—" she snapped her fingers, making him blink out of his heavy-lidded daze "—we're ready."

"I know what you mean."

"So while Allie is… I mean I can tell that she is really fabulous. The kind of person I'd like to be friends with, too." She slid her elbows farther toward him, beckoning him closer. He obliged until their faces were about four inches apart, Sandra gazing rapturously at his boyishly handsome face, Erik gazing rapturously at her cleavage. "But don't you think that you, forever after, night after night, with a woman who isn't dying for it every hour of every day…? I'm just saying."

Erik's eyes jumped up into hers with a fierce, animalistic expression sexy enough to scatter electricity through her.

Sweet mercy.

So that was how he landed his prey. Start with the boy-next-door charm, and get 'em when they're hot.

He edged closer. Two inches apart. Perfect. "I think I'm starting to see your—"

The back door from the porch into the kitchen burst open. Jonas and Allie stood in the doorway, right on glorious cue.

A brief and deliciously awkward silence. Yet again.

"Good morning, Jonas," Sandra said cheerfully.

"Hi, Sandra." He sounded dumbstruck.

"Allie!" Erik, not sure whether to attack or defend.

"Erik…" Allie, looking adorably bemused.

Ta-daaa! What fun.

This weekend was going to turn out even better than she'd hoped.

Julie: So? How is Mr. Hottie this morning?

Allie: We went kayaking. Frolicking happened.

Julie: Frolicking! This is starting to sound serious. How is Erik?

Allie: Sullen. Tell me I have nothing to feel guilty about.

Julie: Guilty? GUILTY? OMG, do not even start with guilty. The guy is a putz. You owe him nada.

Allie: Gotta go, Erik's taking me up to the attic!
Julie: Tie those legs together, girlfriend.

THE CLOTHES WERE better than Allie had hoped. Much better. She
was in heaven, surrounded by four steamer wardrobes. Inside each
were stacked sliding drawers on one side and hanging space on
the other. Erik had hung around hopefully for a while, but after it
became obvious that Allie was completely absorbed in the silks,
velvets, satins and sequins of fashion history and paying him
only grudging attention, he gave up and went back downstairs,
complaining that the attic was getting too hot.

Hot? There was a fan siphoning air out the top of the house,
and with a breeze blowing in through the open windows at either end of the room, Allie found the spot perfectly comfortable
if a bit noisy.

But then, with a treasure trove like this around her, she could
have been sitting on spikes in a lake of boiling oil and been fine.

In the one trunk she'd gone through that morning, one of
Grandmother Bridget's from the 1940s, she'd found a fabulous
array of suits in stunning colors—emerald, gold, coral—with
feminine fitted jackets with contrasting collars and flared pep-
lums. There were knee-length pencil skirts and A-lines that fell
to mid-calf. Full-legged high-waisted pants, blouses with low-cut
necklines and full sleeves with wide cuffs. Hats, scarves, furs…
and gowns! Black satin with a full skirt and Queen Anne neckline. Turquoise silk with silver sequins forming a flame pattern
cinching at the waist. Red velvet with an off-the-shoulder neckline, fitted bodice and a flared skirt. A gold strapless gown with
a sweetheart neckline and matching full-length gold coat.

All of the gowns had *matching shoes!* Allie was ready to weep
with happiness.

Of course not everything was in perfect shape. Some colors
had faded, some spots had developed, the thinnest fabrics were
disintegrating here and there.

Even so, Allie felt as if she'd stepped into the dressing room
on the set of an Edith Head movie. Imagine having so much fin-
ery stashed in the attic of a summer house! Maybe the clothes

were all transferred here when Bridget's year-round house was sold. Maybe she had a whole other wardrobe somewhere else.

It boggled the mind.

The only disappointment was that the clothes were too large to fit her. Erik and Jonas's grandmother must have been a tall, imposing woman. Allie would have to ask to see pictures. Maybe they had shots of her wearing some of the outfits.

She stretched, thinking she should go down for lunch soon, or at least get a glass of water. It was heating up as the sun climbed overhead. She should plan to do her work here in the early mornings.

Or...evenings. Because the early mornings might be her and Jonas's time to cheat on Erik and Sandra.

She rolled her eyes at her own crush-induced idiocy and moved toward the exit, passing an older emerald-green trunk covered with labels of ocean liners and hotels from all over Europe. Was this Great-Grandma Josephine's? What a life she must have led. The Roaring Twenties...

A glance at Allie's watch showed almost noon. Her stomach was growling, but she couldn't leave without a peek inside the trunk, at least. She lifted the lock and undid the clasps, spreading the sides of the trunk to reveal four drawers occupying one half and another bonanza of clothing hung on the other.

She dived in.

Dresses, hats, gloves, costume jewelry, underwear. All from the twenties and thirties. Beaded velvet, green chiffon, elaborate black lace overlays, all wearable, or nearly wearable, after the better part of a century. There must be magic air in this attic.

And lingerie, oh my goodness. Teddies, sheer white nightgowns, tap pants and camisoles, lacy tops, embroidered slips. Best of all, it looked as if Josephine had been much closer to Allie's size than Bridget. She should probably try on some of these things.

As she riffled eagerly through the drawer, she noticed slips of paper pinned to some of the items. On each slip of paper was a neatly handwritten number. Had the clothes been cataloged somewhere? For an exhibit maybe? She checked the dresses and other items for similar markings. Nothing. Just the lingerie had been tagged, and one nightgown, number thirty-five. Thirty-five out of what? Josephine's thirty-fifth nightgown? But then where were one through thirty-four? Maybe she could ask Jonas and Erik about the numbers, though most people didn't know a whole lot about their extended relatives' underwear.

She unfolded nightgown number thirty-five—an impossibly beautiful garment of white cotton batiste, sheer as a veil—and held it up to her body. Intricate floral vines were embroidered in white thread up and down the gown's mid-calf length. Delicate white lace trimmed the hem and sleeves. Tiny silk rosebuds bloomed on the bodice, and silk ribbons tied at each shoulder.

Allie had never seen anything so lovely.

A quick look at the attic trapdoor showed no one. She'd change standing behind the trunk for privacy. Erik had said the clothes were hers, that his mother wanted to get rid of them. It should be fine to try them on.

Nervous and excited, she pulled down her shorts and stripped off her bra and shirt, then carefully pulled the delicate fabric over her head. Thank goodness the threads held—she'd been half-afraid of tearing the garment just by picking it up.

It fit her perfectly. The three-quarter sleeves were narrow, connected to the garment only under the arm, their lacy hem circling her biceps and leaving her shoulders bare. Silk ribbons tied on either side of her neck. Who had seen Josephine in this? Had he untied the ribbons and let it slide down to expose her body?

Allie glanced at the huge heavy-framed mirror leaning against the opposite wall and couldn't resist. Walking carefully, so as not to snag the material on the corner of a trunk or box, she made her way toward the glass, feeling like a siren from the past.

The nightgown looked as if it had been made for her. Her slight tan set off the sheer white and pink beautifully, her eyes shone under her bangs, ruffling in the fan breeze, and for once her plain blond hair didn't seem drab, though she really needed a bob with a Marcel wave and matching rosebuds pinned at her temple. Maybe embroidered slippers.

The only jarring note was the decidedly modern lines of her white bikini underwear. She stepped out of them, imagining that the fabric gave off the faintest smell of rose petals when she moved.

Entranced, she stood at the mirror, imagining Josephine, her life, her loves. Erik said she had five children, a husband who was a writer, and that she was a "party animal." Did her husband buy her such beautiful things and plead with her to model them? Did Josephine buy them herself and surprise him? Did she own any of them before she was married? Did any other men see them on her? How many?

Allie ran her hands up and down the soft sheer material, thinking she should go down to lunch before someone missed her and came calling.

She turned from the mirror and was about to bend over to pick up her panties when she stopped dead.

Jonas was sticking his head through the trapdoor, looking as if he'd seen…a naked woman. He had that look all men get, that sort of glazed tongue-hanging-out thing.

She was about to panic, duck down or try to cover herself when calm descended over her. Okay. He'd seen her body. Nakedness was not a disease, nor was it evil. And heaven knew she'd been fantasizing pretty much nonstop about showing hers to him. She could act as if this was a terrible, embarrassing mistake.

Or go with it.

"Hey, Jonas. What's up?"

"I'm…I'd…I came up to—" He gave up and stood there, looking her up and down.

"Isn't this beautiful?" She gestured to the gown. "It's one of your great-grandmother's nightgowns. I couldn't resist trying it on."

"It's beautiful, Allie." Apparently he'd found his voice. And he no longer looked as if he'd swallowed a gnat. In fact his eyes were heating up to a dark blue smolder. "And you look amazing in it."

"Thank you." She smiled as if he'd complimented her on a new backpack. "Lunch happening any time soon?"

"Yes, it's ready. I came up to tell you…" His look clearly finished the sentence. *And I got a lot more than I bargained for.*

"Great. I'll be down as soon as I change. I'm starving after our ride this morning."

"Funny. I didn't realize how hungry I was." He gave the night-gown another slow, thorough perusal. "Until now."

CHAPTER SIX

JONAS STRODE UP the stairs of the main house and knocked gently on Sandra's door, hoping she wasn't taking a nap. He needed to talk to her.

"Yeah, who is it?"

"Jonas."

"Jonas, my darling, come in."

He pushed open the door cautiously, hoping his notoriously immodest friend wasn't half-dressed. He and Sandra kept few secrets from each other, but he'd seen the only naked body he wanted to see right before lunch, and life would just get out-of-control confusing if he was faced with another one so soon after.

Sandra was standing by the window, looking fabulously sexy in a black-and-white bikini. Sort of naked, but Jonas could handle it. He gave a whistle and leered inappropriately, knowing she wouldn't take him seriously. "Oh baby, my fire is lit."

"Yeah, snuff it. What's on your mind?" She grabbed a beach towel from the bed and slipped her feet into flip-flops. "As if I didn't know."

"You do, huh?" He put his hands on his hips, figuring she probably did. Tension at lunch had been thick enough to strangle most conversation. Sandra had saved them, chatting easily, while undoubtedly missing nothing. "I'm going on a hike, want to come with me?"

Sandra snorted and gave him a look as if he'd just suggested lava-surfing. "Take a guess."

"A walk, then. Easy."

She gestured to her outfit, or near lack thereof. "Listen, honey, it's eighty degrees and the sun is shining. This body is moving only to turn over to bake its other side. Possibly to enter the lake to cool off. Then repeat. This is what bodies are made to do in the summertime at the beach. Got it?"

"Yes, ma'am." He grinned at her. "Okay if I join you?"

She pretended to consider. "Will you rub suntan lotion on my back and fetch iced tea when I require it?"

"Absolutely."

"Okay. Let's go." She started toward him, wrapping the towel around her waist. "I take it you need to talk?"

"Might be a good idea."

"For everyone up here." As they fell into step she gave his arm a sympathetic squeeze. "Don't worry, I'll be the easiest. Go put on a suit, I'll meet you at the beach."

He changed into his bathing suit and joined Sandra, settling beside her near the water. She had a point about the beach today. The temperature was perfect, the sun's heat tempered by a steady breeze that also kept away insects.

"First, my lover." She held out the lotion. "We must always use protection."

He spread the cream onto her back, keeping his touch impersonal without any effort. His head was so full of Allie that he wasn't tuned into Sandra's body the way he usually was. It was quite a body, too—narrow waist, flat stomach, full breasts and curving hips. A real woman's body, one he'd enjoyed a lot. But the sight of Allie, hazel eyes shining, cheeks flushed, standing proudly, her nakedness barely hidden by material so transparent it didn't seem possible it could hold together, had taken over his brain in an all-out assault. The combination of sexuality and sweetness had nearly undone him. He had no idea how he'd managed to get through lunch.

Luckily, his brain had enough sense left in it to realize that if he wanted her…no, that wasn't the question. He wanted her so badly he'd been half-erect for the last two hours. But before he acted, there were two people he cared about deeply who'd need to be okay with him and Allie getting together.

"So." He took off his shirt and started spreading lotion on himself. "Talk time."

"Yes, it's okay with me if you and Allie screw like possessed bunnies." She lay back on her towel and exhaled blissfully. "God, it's fabulous out. Why in hell haven't you brought me up here before this?"

He recovered from his surprise. "That's it?"

"What's it?"

"Come on, Sandra."

"What do you want me to say? No, no, please don't be with her, I couldn't bear it, my heart would shatter into a million—"

"Sure, why not?" As usual she'd nailed him. Sandra didn't tolerate male ego. Or female, but that didn't apply to him so he didn't care. Since that intolerance was one of the things he respected about her, he'd better not get pissed off about it now that it was directed at him.

"Dream on." She reached over and smacked his arm. "You know how I feel about you. I adore you. And I know we both talked about things working out ultimately between us. But in the meantime, we both have full license to try to find someone more suitable. So you need to do what you need to do."

"It won't bother you?"

She turned to him, lowering her sunglasses and peering at him over their bright red frames. "Would it bother you if our situations were reversed and you thought I had a real chance to be happy?"

He narrowed his eyes, turning that one over, remembering her face inches from Erik's. "Well…no. But I wouldn't want to watch."

"Exactly." Sandra pushed her glasses back up. "I will not suffer, I promise you that. Your happiness is important to me. And Allie seems fabulous. Okay? Are we good now?"

He leaned over and kissed her cocoa-buttery cheek. "We are good."

"Next item."

"Yeah." Jonas settled back onto the sand. "Erik."

"Mmm, you leave him to me."

He gave a startled laugh. "What do you mean?"

"I have plans for Erik."

A queasy feeling started in Jonas's stomach. "What kind of plans?"

"Plans that will make him forget he ever wanted your Allie."

He felt a sting of jealousy. "Jeez, Sandra, you're going to sleep with my brother?"

"No one's asking you to watch." She repositioned her head, smiling smugly. "Maybe yes, maybe no. But I'm definitely going to make him desperate to sleep with me."

"How are you going to—" He shook his head, trying to process the concept of Sandra going after his brother. "Never mind, I don't want to know."

"Smart boy."

"But I do want to know one thing."

"Mmm?" She turned her face more directly toward the sun.

"Why are you doing this? So I can be with Allie?"

"Ha!" Her brows drew down disdainfully. "Do I look like Pollyanna?"

"Uh, no, that's why I'm asking."

"It's a chick thing," she said primly.

Jonas made a growling sound. "Meaning I wouldn't understand because I have male equipment."

"Exactly."

"Which means whatever it is, it makes no sense."

"Not to you, no."

"Okay, okay, have your private babe club. I still have to talk to Erik, though." He brightened. "Hey, if he gives up on Allie willingly, you won't have to torment him on my account."

"Yes, I will." She stretched her soft arms above her head and let them drop. "But you wouldn't understand that, either."

"I'm sure I wouldn't." He rolled his eyes, wondering if on some weird level, Sandra actually liked his brother. Was that possible? He didn't see why not. Guys a lot more horrible than Erik had been happily paired off. Erik just needed grounding. And to grow up a little. Maybe Sandra could make that happen. Jonas wouldn't put anything past her.

He spent another half hour enjoying the sun until he heard Erik's car returning from town where he'd taken Allie to buy groceries. If Allie disappeared back up into the attic, Jonas would get the chance to talk to Erik alone.

Allie's laugh floated down from the parking area. His heart beating faster, Jonas got up and walked toward them, pulling his shirt back on. "Need help?"

"Nah, we're fine." His brother wasn't overtly hostile, but Jonas could sense his annoyance. You grew up with someone, you got pretty good at reading him.

"If you want to get back to the attic, Allie, I can help Erik unload."

"Oh, I don't mind helping." She glanced uncertainly at Erik, looking as girlish in her crazy peacock shorts as she had looked womanly in the lingerie upstairs.

"Go on." Jonas went to take the groceries from her, gave her a quick nod and tipped his head pointedly toward Erik, hoping she'd understand.

She gave a quick nod back and released the bag. "If you're sure, I'd love to get back up there. I have a mystery to solve."

"Really." He had to make himself move toward the house or he would have stood there gazing at her like a fool. "What kind of mystery?"

"In one of your great-grandmother's trunks some of the clothes have tags with numbers on them."

Erik looked disappointed. "That's your mystery?"

"I was hoping for a treasure map," Jonas said.

"Men." Allie laughed and held the door open for him and Erik, then left them to unload the groceries in the kitchen and hurried upstairs.

"So, Erik." Jonas pulled out a bag of sweet-corn ears and laid it on the counter. "Looks like we have a complicated situation here."

"Yeah?" Erik put away a couple of fabulous-looking steaks, not meeting his brother's eye, his jaw set.

Jonas gritted his teeth. He wasn't going to make this easy. "With you and me, Sandra and Allie."

"How so?"

"Cut the crap. We need to talk about this."

"I don't have anything I need to talk about. If you have a problem, feel free to tell me what it is."

Jonas took out a couple of bottles of sparkling water and barely resisted throwing them at his brother's head. "Okay, Erik. Here's my problem. There's something happening between Allie and me, and I don't feel I can do anything about it unless you and I talk it out."

"What about Sandra?"

"She's fine with it."

His face twisted into skepticism. "She's *fine* with it?"

Jonas sighed, calling on his patience. He was really getting tired of his brother's drama. "I talked to her just now. She's fine with it."

Erik shrugged and unloaded a bag of mixed lettuces, but he seemed less cranky all of a sudden. "Good for her."

"She gets that this is nothing I planned or expected, it's just how things worked out."

"Well, ain't she a saint."

"I prefer the term goddess." Sandra sauntered into the room, looking incredibly hot in her bikini, bringing with her the scent of cocoa butter and woman. Erik froze holding a bag of chips in midair, his mouth half-open, eyes slightly bulging. Jonas suppressed a grin. He'd bet that was exactly how he'd looked faced with Allie in the barely-there nightie.

"Hey, goddess," he said.

"Having fun?" She shot Jonas a look of sympathy and grabbed a diet soda from the refrigerator. "You being a good boy, Erik?"

Erik sent her a look of disgust.

"I'll tell you something." She stood close to him, near-naked body leaning casually against the counter about a foot from his, their heads nearly the same height. The soda can whooshed, then clicked. She took a long drink, head thrown back. Erik's Adam apple bobbed convulsively. The chips were still suspended in his grip. "You've lost already, and you know it as well as anyone. Fighting now just makes you look like a jerk."

Jonas held his breath, not sure whether to groan or crack up. In a few words she'd said exactly what he probably would have taken the rest of the afternoon trying to put as tactfully and inoffensively as possible. Erik still would have taken offense. The joys of family baggage.

Erik's eyes narrowed. He looked murderous. Sandra gave him

a sweet smile and reached up to press a kiss to his cheek, making his eyes shoot wide and the fight leave his body.

"There." Sandra trailed a red-nailed hand lingeringly across his jaw. "All better. Easy, huh?"

She turned, threw Jonas a conspirator's wink, then sauntered out of the kitchen in that way that ensured he and Erik could do nothing but watch until she was out of sight and their higher motor functions resumed.

"What was *that?*" Erik still looked stunned.

Jonas chuckled and slapped him on the back, relieved when Erik shook himself comically. This was going to be okay. "That was a combination centerfold and freight train."

"I think I was just put in my place."

"But *so* attractively."

Erik laughed nervously, but at least he was laughing. Then he gave a great sigh of reluctant surrender. "Okay, well, if she's left us anything to talk about, I guess we should talk."

Allie: Jonas saw me wearing a see-through outfit today. I think he wasn't miserable about what he saw. Nothing left to the imagination.

Julie: Trust me, he was imagining plenty. How's Erik while all this lusting is going on?

Allie: I'm wondering if there's something about to happen with him and Sandra.

Julie: Gah! You guys could be on a reality show!

ALLIE REACHED for the last drawer on Great-Grandmother Josephine's trunk, wondering what Erik and Jonas were talking about downstairs—if she'd read Jonas's signals right and that was what they were doing. She shouldn't guess and she shouldn't hope, but of course she was doing both.

In the meantime…she opened the drawer with eager anticipation, hardly able to believe that all these wonderful clothes belonged to her. She'd never in her life owned anything remotely as fabulous. The knowledge made her a bit giddy.

What would she find this time? More jewelry? Gloves?

Books.

Why here? The house was full of books, and there were a few boxes up in the attic marked "books", as well. Maybe these were special to Josephine. Maybe they'd be particularly valuable titles—a Fitzgerald or Hemingway first edition? If that were the case, she'd be sure to return them to Jonas and Erik. Her gift had involved only clothing items.

She picked up one volume from the stack on the right…no title on the cover. Inside, she found handwriting on paper browning with age.

A diary.

Her heart beating faster, she turned the pages. The writing was cramped and shaky. 1968 to 1971. Josephine would have been an older woman then.

She dug down to the bottom of the pile on the far left. The writing in this journal was larger and much more awkward. 1908 to 1912. *My name is Josephine and I am eight years old.*

Allie clutched the slim volume to her chest. The rest of the diaries must fall between those two. A lifetime—her travels, her adventures, first kiss, first love, meeting and marrying her husband, her children's births—all that could be in these books, and more. Did Erik and Jonas know they existed? They should have them, an incredible record of their ancestor's life and thoughts. A detailed slice of Meyer family history.

She flipped through the first few books beginning to end, turning clumps of pages, reading a line or two here and there. Nothing earthshaking. A new dress. A visit to a friend. Complaints about schoolwork. Parties with best friends. Something cute her dog did.

But who was Josephine when she was wearing these clothes? Who was she when she was closer to Allie's age? Allie fingered the stack of mostly black, navy and green volumes, then picked out a burgundy one—the only red shade—in what she estimated was the bottom third of the chronology.

1923 to 1927. Perfect.

She opened the book and leafed through, noticing that in this volume, unlike the other two, the pages were numbered, top center, in thick black ink. Every now and then, a page number was circled. Incredibly curious, she leafed back to read the first one she'd noticed: page twenty-four.

My dear diary, if I play this right, my spinster years will be over soon. At Smith, they taught us to think and to question, but I've discovered that men only want women who'll obey and agree. However, last week I met Walter Alden, another son of friends of Mum and Daddy's coming to Lake George to stay with us. Funny how many of these unmarried dullards seem to show up. I was dreading his arrival as usual. But what a surprise! Halfway through the main course at dinner I realized the problem with my theory. Yes, boys want submissive women. But men don't. Before Walter, I'd only been meeting boys. By the time dessert was served that first night, I knew I wanted him. All that was left was convincing him he simply must marry me.

I started by getting him alone as much as possible (of course Mum and Daddy were delighted), then I'd act as if I couldn't care less whether he lived or died. That didn't work. So I tried subtle flirting instead. He responded just fine, but remained polite and respectful. I didn't want polite and respectful. I wanted to know if the kisses of a man would bore me as much as the kisses of a boy.

I suspected not.

Desperate times… Last night I sneaked out to the cottage with a bottle of champagne and a couple of glasses. "What's this for?" he said. "Does it have to be for anything?" I answered. We drank a good deal of the bottle, having a really nice talk, then calm as you please, practically in the middle of his sentence, I stood up and took off my dress. Under it, I was wearing only silk and my sheerest stockings. I sat back down as if nothing had happened and picked up my champagne again.

I'll never forget his face as long as I live.

Yes, the kisses of a man are different.

Allie blinked up from the entry. Go, Josephine! Maybe this was more than Jonas and Erik wanted to know about Great-Grandma. Allie wished she could have seen her in action. Had the sexy silk she was wearing survived? Was it here in one of the trunks or somewhere else?

Staring down at the page—the number twenty-four, circled—something clicked. She scrambled to her feet and pawed through the lingerie, looking at tags. Twenty-four. The pink tap pants and camisole combination. Silk.

Coincidence?

Turning sharply to the other side of the trunk, she rummaged through the rack of hanging clothes and extracted the sheer night-gown Jonas had seen pretty much all of her in. Hands trembling, she smoothed out the label. Thirty-five.

Back to the diary. She leafed through quickly—twenty-eight, thirty-four...

"Hellooo?" Sandra's voice, coming up the stairs. "Anyone home?"

Shoot!

"I'm here." Allie shoved the books back in the drawer and closed it, instinctively wanting to keep her discovery secret for at least a while longer. Certainly Jonas or Erik should hear about the diaries before Sandra did. "Come on up."

"On my way." Her head poked up over the floor level, then the rest of her followed, flushed from sunbathing, hair wet from a recent shower. She was disgustingly poised and gorgeous, one of those people who made Allie feel her dowdy Brooklyn roots were showing. No wonder Jonas—

Nope. She wasn't going to think about that.

"Wow, it's amazing up here." Sandra wrinkled her nose. "And hot. But not as bad as I expected."

"No, it's not bad with the fan going. Worth it, anyway. Look at this stuff." Allie steered her to Grandma Bridget's trunk, not only protecting Josephine's diaries, but also because those clothes might fit Sandra where they'd flopped forlornly on Allie's body. Inversely, Josephine's flapper dresses suited Allie perfectly, but wouldn't be able to handle Sandra's height or curves.

"Oh my sweet heaven, would you look at these clothes!" She took out a royal-blue satin gown and held it up. "Why can't we dress this way anymore?"

"I know. Except clothes of this quality would be prohibitively expensive now."

"Hey, let someone else pay. Then point me to Goodwill and let me at 'em." Holding the dress high to keep the hem off the dusty floor, she walked over to the mirror and posed this way and that.

"Try it on."

"Can I?"

"Sure, Erik said I could have the clothes, so it's up to me."

"Oooh, too fabulous, thank you." She dropped her shorts and hauled off her shirt in about ten seconds. Under it she wore a purple lace bra-and-panty set—the kind of thing Josephine would be collecting by the crate if she were alive today. Allie cringed at the thought of her mismatched plain underwear. Clearly she'd missed one of the joys of the classy, sensual woman. "I came up to talk to you."

"Okay." Allie watched her, uncomfortable at the thought of what she might be about to say. "Stay away from Jonas or die" came to mind.

"Just had an interesting talk with the adorable Meyer brothers." She pulled the dress over her head.

"About…"

"You."

"Me?" She folded her arms across her chest, feeling undressed herself. What would the three of them have to say about her?

"Oh la *la*. Would you look at *this!*" Sandra put her arms through the gathered cap sleeves and zipped up the dress, which fit as though it was made for her. She looked incredible. Jonas could not be allowed to see her like that.

"The dress is totally you." Allie smiled approvingly, hoping Sandra would get back on topic.

"I feel like a movie star!" Sandra did a three-sixty, craning to look at the plunging vee in the back. "No wonder you're up here all the time."

"Yeah, it's been amazing. There are tons more gowns, all gorgeous and most in perfect condition."

"Fantabulous." She spread her arms wide, curtseyed to her reflection, mimed waltzing.

Allie's smile grew tired. "So, um, what did—"

"I've noticed what's happening between you and Jonas." Sandra stopped dancing, catching Allie's eye in the mirror. "So has Erik."

"Nothing is actually happening." Allie stood stiffly, praying Sandra believed her.

The other woman turned, her gaze frank but not angry, unless she was good at hiding her feelings and would soon explode in a prima-donna rage. "You know what I mean."

Allie bent her head, sort of a nod, sort of not. Until she could figure out Sandra's mood, and whether there were any fire axes or old swords in her vicinity, she wouldn't be sure how to handle this.

"The upshot of the conversation was that Erik realizes he's being a dork. That you're not into him and he's stupid to hold out hope."

Allie's head jerked up. "He said all that?"

"Of course not." Sandra, back at the mirror, gathered her long dark hair into a French twist and held it behind her head. "But it's what he thinks. He just hasn't come around to admitting it yet."

"Oh." Allie's heart gave a tiny leap. Where was this going? She hardly dared guess.

"And I assume Jonas told you there is nothing going on between us but friendship. Or he might not have. He can get awkward around complicated feelings."

Complicated feelings? For Allie or for Sandra? Allie was getting impatient. "Would you mind telling me exactly what you're trying to say?"

"I'm saying…" Sandra lifted the dress's hem and turned back and forth, making the material swirl around her ankles. "Let nothing stand in the way of you pursuing some very fine Jon-ass."

Allie broke into a short laugh. "Just like that?"

"What?" Sandra turned in exasperation. "You need it in writing?"

Allie gritted her teeth. Okay, she deserved that. It probably wasn't easy for Sandra to come up here, given her past with Jonas, and it was incredibly nice of her to step out of the way. Allie should be gracious about it. "Thank you for telling me, Sandra. If you're sure you'll be okay with it. And if you're sure Erik—"

"I'll take care of Erik." She smiled at herself in the mirror, a small smile, almost dreamy. "By the time I am through with him, he'll forget you ever existed."

Allie burst out laughing, delighted when Sandra giggled along with her. "You like him?"

"That man needs to be taught a lesson. I just happen to be a very willing teacher." She took the dress off with obvious reluctance. "Can I come up and try some other stuff on sometime?"

"Sure, of course, anytime." She nodded too many times, liar that she was, preferring privacy. "I still have other trunks to go through."

"Excellent." Sandra stepped into her shorts and pulled her tank top back over her head. "Dinner will be ready around seven, but they're pouring gin and tonics at six."

"I can live with that."

"Yeah, this life is not exactly a hardship." She passed close to Allie and touched her arm. She smelled faintly of ginger and something sweeter. "Be nice to Jonas. He's a good guy."

Allie nodded, strangely emotional. "I promise."

She watched Sandra descend the ladder, then hauled out her phone, adrenaline rushing. Julie needed to hear about this. They'd have to plan how this would go, how she and Jonas would get together, who'd take the lead, when, where…

Halfway through her text, she stopped. Wait a second.

She didn't need to ask herself or Julie any of those questions. Great-Grandma Josephine had not only sketched out various seductions, but had also provided all the outfits. Allie gave a slow, wicked grin, envisioning some very specific erotic pleasures.

Tonight, Jonas would be subjected to a full treatment of page twenty-four.

CHAPTER SEVEN

Allie: Just finished dinner. Champagne on ice. Getting ready.

Julie: I get Diet Coke, you get champagne. No fair. Is it hot there?

Allie: Not as hot as it's about to get, heh heh.

Julie: Sweltering here. Subway smells like the pee of ten thousand frat boys. Don't come back!

Allie: You're not exactly tempting me.

ALLIE TOOK HER TIME getting ready, immersing herself in the mood she wanted to create, moving languidly, not allowing her breathing to accelerate, aiming for a dreamy, sensual state she could bring with her to the cottage, and to Jonas. She was also bringing champagne, which she'd pilfered from the generous stash in the bar refrigerator, making a note to replace the bottle next time she was in town, though it would probably never be missed. Not sure how well outfitted the cottage was, she'd also grabbed glasses and an ice bucket.

Allie showered, shaved, applied lotion, plucked and trimmed, then put on the thin flowered robe that had been hanging in her room's closet, and floated down the hall back to her room. Inside, she crossed to the open window and let the robe fall and the breeze off the lake caress her body, gently finger-combing her hair from bottom to top, wet strands sliding through her fingers.

Erik and Sandra's laughter drifted up from the kitchen. After a delicious and relaxed meal on the screened-in porch, talk had grown increasingly sparse until it became obvious they were all trying to figure out how to split into couples with the least amount of awkwardness. Finally, Jonas had stepped in with a really funny and tactful job of saying they'd undoubtedly not see each other for the rest of the night.

What was Jonas doing right now? Lying in bed? Looking out at the water? Sitting on the beach?

How would he react to Josephine's plan?

She couldn't wait to find out.

The pink tap pants and camisole from page twenty-four of the diary had been hanging on the door opposite the window to freshen them, though contrary to what she'd expected, there was little to no musty smell.

The camisole—very plainly designed, and probably considered a bra in the twenties—was trimmed with cream-colored lace and ended mid-stomach, leaving some room for the imagination. The style was tight, designed to flatten a woman's bosom in order to produce the era's ideal boyish figure. The tops of Allie's breasts were visible above the lace and her nipples felt exquisite against the smooth, slippery silk. The tap pants skimmed the outline of her buttocks. A tiny silk rosebud wreath had been stitched in the center of the camisole, and another nestled in a patch of lace on the hem of the panties' right leg. The outfit made her look lean, feminine, and ultrasophisticated. Tonight no one would mistake her for a girl from a rough part of Brooklyn's Kensington neighborhood.

Over the lingerie, she pulled one of the simplest dresses from Josephine's wardrobe: a cream-colored linen sheath lined with peach silk that peeked through a lacy network of floral cutouts from shoulder to waist.

On her feet—she didn't bother with stockings—she wore a pair of cream-colored shoes with low heels and cutouts by the button fastener for the strap.

One last look in the mirror as she perched a cream cloche-style hat on her head.

There.

Allie smiled at her reflection. The outfit not only felt entirely comfortable, but also entirely her—not as if she was dressing up in a costume from another era—but as if she was putting on an outfit bought for herself. Maybe it was her longtime obsession with vintage clothes, but clearly she was at ease indulging a spectacular *Great Gatsby* moment. And why not?

She liked her own century very much, thanks, with progress on women's issues and advances in health care, but she'd love to have experienced the exuberance of the 1920s. Especially as someone with Josephine's money, class and confidence. This woman could meet the queen of England and not have a thing to hide.

Turning away from the mirror, Allie scooped up the ice bucket and glasses and headed for the door, her steps firm, her mind clear and directed, channeling Josephine's quest to seduce Walter. Except Allie wasn't after marriage. Someday she'd find a man who had worked as hard as she had to build a successful life, who understood where she'd been and why it was so important to her to get out. Together, they'd build a true partnership. On this quest, however, she was quite happy to settle for Jonas's superb body.

Passing the kitchen as quietly as possible, she overheard Erik and Sandra having what sounded like an earnest discussion. Out in the fading light, she walked the straight line to the cottage leisurely and purposefully. At the door, she knocked and took a step back, calm smile in place.

Where had she gotten this much sangfroid? This much courage? She'd spent most of her adult life pretending she was more refined than she was, but never to this degree. Plus, she was about to seduce a man she barely knew—a calm, conscious decision, made in hot blood. Allie had never come close to doing something like this. Maybe the clothes had turned her into a new woman?

Never mind. She had the courage, and she was loving every second of it. That was all she needed to know.

"Hey, the party's arrived." Jonas's surprise gave way to a thorough inspection and a slow, appreciative grin. "Wow. Look at you. You're beautiful. It's as if that outfit was made for you."

"Thank you." She held his gaze, a cool smile in place, though her cheeks were warming with pleasure at his compliment. He must have just showered. Damp, dark hair curled around his face, his blue eyes vivid against skin warmed by the sun. Around his mouth and on his cheeks, the barest hint of beard showed he'd shaved for their after-dinner date. He wore loose, comfortable shorts and an unbuttoned blue-and-white patterned shirt through which his very nice chest showed.

"Guess I'm underdressed." He backed into the cottage, buttoning his shirt. She thought about stopping him, but decided it would be more fun to unbutton it herself again later. "Come on in. I was about to pull out beer for us, but for some strange reason I'm now thinking champagne…"

"Me, too. Same strange reason I bet." She let him take the bucket. "Can we sit out on the deck?"

"Absolutely, Ms. McDonald. It's a beautiful night. Though there's not much room out there for the Charleston." He led the way through the sliding door out onto the deck and set the bucket on the table. Perfect. They had a fabulous view of the lake, but Sandra and Erik couldn't see them from the house unless they came down to the beach, which was unlikely.

Jonas removed the bottle from its ice bedding and began twisting off the cage, staring at her the whole time. "Is it okay if I can't take my eyes off you?"

"I think it's fine." She made a slow turn to show off the dress. When she came around again, Jonas was still holding the bottle, having made no progress opening it.

Oh, this was going to be fun.

"Need help with the cork?" she asked sweetly.

"Uh, no." He busied himself again. "But men's brains can only handle one thing at a time. Where are Erik and Sandra?"

"Talking in the kitchen. Sounded pretty intense."

His left eyebrow rose. "I have a feeling they'll be busy for quite a while."

"I have that same feeling." She watched him for signs of emotion, but he seemed calm about Sandra pairing off with his brother.

Good thing.

The cork came out with a soft pop, followed by a wisp of mist that looked like smoke. Jonas expertly poured the foaming gold into the glasses and handed her one. "Here's to a beautiful night with a beautiful woman who has apparently time-traveled to be with me."

"She has." Allie sipped the cool, bubbly heaven, and sat gracefully in the chair he held out for her. "Your great-grandmother was quite the woman."

"That's what Grandma Bridget always told us. What made you think so?"

"Diaries. A pile of them." Allie crossed her feet demurely at the ankles and sipped her champagne, which was so much better than the stuff she bought that she was retroactively embarrassed. "She kept one her whole life. Did you know?"

"No, I didn't."

"You and Erik should take a look. I hope it's okay that I've been reading them."

"Sure." He was watching her with a glint of warm amusement in his eyes. "What are you finding out about her?"

"She was a very smart woman. Very practical. Strong." She sent Jonas a coy look from under her hat brim. "Very sexual."

"Really." He looked pained. "Do I want to know this about a relative?"

"She was quite the se-duc-tress." Allie enunciated carefully, forming her lips and tongue around the word, giving it sensual weight.

The pained look dissipated; his gaze intensified. "Was she?"

"I learned quite a bit."

"Tell me." His voice turned husky.

"For example." She took off the cloche, shook out her hair leisurely, enjoying the cool breeze on her scalp. "It's a good idea to make a man want you until he can't think of anything else."

Jonas didn't move. His eyes were trying to hold her prisoner.

"After that." Allie blinked to break his power, saying a short prayer that she could pull this off as beautifully as she'd bet Josephine had. "You offer yourself, but only so far."

"Because…"

"The big prize waits until you're sure you have him." She slowly pulled down the zipper in the side of the dress. "Until you get what you want."

He swallowed, his eyes following her movements. "What did she want?"

"Marriage." Allie stood, took hold of the hem of the dress and pulled it up and over her head, matter-of-factly turning it back right-side out and draping it carefully over the back of her chair. Then she sat again, leaning back, crossing her legs, and picked up her champagne again. "But I'm just after tonight."

He was devouring her with his eyes, the swell of her breasts under the camisole, the length of her thigh emerging from the pink silk. "I can do that."

She suppressed a laugh at his eagerness, tipped up her face, eyes closed, and let her hair stream back in the sudden breeze, enjoying the anticipation, her power, his desire, sending a thank-you up to Josephine who she hoped was watching, cheering her on.

Then she opened her eyes and smiled in pure happiness at the look on Jonas's face. What woman didn't want a crazy-hot man going brain-dead with lust over her?

His gaze darkened suspiciously. "You're enjoying this, aren't you?"

"Of course." Allie feigned surprise. "Aren't you?"

"Nope." He shook his head, glancing down at his erection, clearly and impressively visible in his shorts. "I'm in agony."

"Good things come to those who wait." Her slight emphasis on "come" wasn't wasted on him.

"You're a good thing. I'm waiting." He pushed his chair back from the table, and spread his arms. "*Come* to me."

Allie considered him gravely, then stood and walked to the railing, gazing out at the lake. "I'm not sure I'm ready to come yet."

"Cruel woman."

"You must be strong." She leaned forward so her backside presented itself provocatively. He groaned. Allie had to hide a giggle. "Lovely view, don't you think?"

"You have no idea."

She peeked at him over her shoulder, shifting her hips to one side. "Poor, poor man."

"This is very hard, Allie."

"I can see that." She straightened and strolled toward him, forcing her breath to stay even. Her body wasn't any more immune to this game than his. Well, maybe a little—he was a guy, after all. "Maybe I can help you."

"Please. Yes, please."

Allie stopped between his parted knees. His hands gripped her bare waist; he looked up at her with a combination of amusement and pleading. Of course he could take control of this situation any time he wanted to, having the physical advantage. But he seemed willing to play along, at least for now.

Slowly, she lifted one thigh outside of his, then the other, sinking down, inch by tantalizing inch, until she felt the hard bulge of his erection touch, then press, against the soft silk between her legs.

His breath exploded out. Allie managed to control her reaction, but only barely. He felt so, so good.

Slowly. Don't give it all away.

"Better?" She braced her hands against his hard chest.

He grunted, moving his hands around to clasp her buttocks. "Depends on how you define better."

"Less pain?"

"More." He pushed his hips up. "Much more."

"Oh, dear." Allie moved her hands to his shoulders and leaned forward to look him in the eyes. "Is it the feel of me against your cock that is causing you this pain?"

"Yes." He spoke tightly, eyes roaming her face, landing briefly on her mouth, and then rushing down to take in her nipples pushing out the pink silk. His hands gripped her harder.

"Would you rather be inside me? With me hot and wet around you? Holding you tight?" Her breathless whisper was an inch from his mouth. "Is that what you want?"

"Yes." His eyes closed; he was fighting for control. "Yes."

"I don't know, Jonas. I hardly know you." She closed the last inch between them, brushed her mouth across his bottom lip, then back along the top. "Let's start here."

His lips were soft, responsive, warm. She closed her eyes to concentrate on their shape, their taste, the change between the moist curves of his mouth and the smooth skin of his cheeks and chin, delicious contact that shot shivers through her body.

He let her keep leading the pace and their movements. Jonas Meyer, who would recoil in horror if he saw the closet she slept in as a child, the neighborhood she grew up in. This man, who had all the power associated with his wealth, breeding and connections, was leaving little Brooklyn Allie in control.

Very gradually, she started to rock back and forth over the thin fabric of his shorts, continuing to explore his mouth, without kissing him full-on or deeply. *Always hold something back.*

Jonas inhaled through his teeth, gripped her hips and helped her along. Allie let her head drop back, riding him, eyes still closed, taking her pleasure from rubbing her clitoris against his hard length through the soft, slippery silk, bringing her close to coming in only a few minutes.

"Allie." He bent forward and murmured against her throat. "You're making me crazy."

You're making me crazy, too.

She had to work harder and harder to appear calm. Her breath caught in little gasps and her thighs began to tremble. She was going to come before he did. Not the plan. Not what was supposed to—

To hell with the plan.

Her orgasm came on slowly, gaining intensity. She gasped openly now, caught up in the intense pleasure, no longer caring if she appeared desperate, rubbing herself back and forth over his erection until her body gathered itself powerfully and she gave in to the rush, suspended in ecstasy that made her bite back a cry, opening her eyes wide, vaginal muscles contracting over and over, pleasure still pulsing intensely.

Jonas let out a curse, pushed against her once, twice, and then gave a low shout. She watched him coming, his eyes closed, mouth half-open in ecstasy, muscles straining.

Then he opened those startlingly blue eyes and they stared at each other in awe for several seconds, breathing hard. Just as she was mortified to find herself about to giggle, he started laughing, too, and the atmosphere became as relaxed and innocently giddy as it had been intensely sexual seconds before.

"Look what you did to me." He gestured down at his stained shorts, still grinning. "I haven't come in my pants since I was a teenager. It's embarrassing."

"No, no, it's not at all. It's completely fine." She lifted herself off him, her legs unsteady, and stood, unable to stop beaming. Mission accomplished. The seduction had been perfect. She'd never felt so on top of the world in her life. "No apologies."

"Allie." He caught her hand, chuckled again. "That was incredible. In our culture, with all the sex around us, we've lost the art and sexiness of subtlety. Thank you for that."

"I'm glad you enjoyed it." She smiled down at him. Around them the sky was darkening, the breeze subsiding to an occasional caress. "I did, too."

Jonas's wide smile faded. He stood, leaned down and touched his lips to hers, then kissed her lingeringly, putting his hand to the side of her face as if she were something precious. "I'll be right back."

Allie stepped back, nodding. Her throat had gone thick; she wasn't sure she'd be able to speak. Turning, she grasped the deck railing and stared out at the lake, deep navy in the twilight, and told herself to get a grip, not to ruin a pure sexual encounter with any silly mooning. She'd just accept the emotion for what it was— inappropriate romanticism—and quietly put it away.

The temperature had dropped some, but not enough to explain her sudden need to cover up again. She pulled the dress back over her head, feeling warmer, yes, but also safer, once more cool and confident. When Jonas came back out in clean shorts, carrying two blankets, she was even able to smile brightly.

"You sleeping under the stars tonight?"

"Want to join me?"

Sleeping in his arms all night out on the beach? She'd wake up stiff, cold and even more infatuated. "I don't think so, but thanks."

He nodded as if he'd been expecting her refusal. "Don't want to give away the farm?"

She laughed, relieved and touched by his easy acceptance. "That's what Josephine would say."

"Would you like to lie on the beach for just a while to watch the stars that we won't be sleeping under?"

"I'd love that."

"Good." He handed her a T-shirt and a pair of shorts. "I brought these if you'd like to rejoin our not-so-stylish but machine-washable century."

"I think that's a good idea." She took the clothes from him. "I'll change in the house."

Immediately, she felt like an idiot. They'd just gone crazy on each other, and she was modest now?

"No, no, stay here. I'll take the blankets down to the beach. I promise, no peeking." He hoisted the blankets and stepped off the deck. "Maybe."

Allie laughed. "I'll bring the champagne with me."

"Excellent idea." He walked down toward the water, then whipped his head around as if hoping to catch her undressed.

"Hey! Eyes forward, soldier!"

She undressed and dressed quickly, watching him not because she was worried he'd peek again, but because his broad shoulders and most stunning butt were so appealing, and the way his tall body moved gracefully across the sand was a real pleasure.

When she arrived at the water's edge with the champagne and glasses, naked under the T-shirt and drawstring shorts, which were threatening to fall at any second, Jonas had already spread the blanket and was lying comfortably on it, hands clasped behind his head.

"Champagne service! This hotel has everything."

"Yes sir." She nodded somberly, thinking these roles were more suited to who they really were. "I hope you have been pleased with my service and will remember my twelve children and unemployed drunk husband."

"Tough break. You poor thing." He patted the blanket next to him. "Maybe I can make it all better."

"Thank you, sir." She nestled the bucket in the sand and poured them each a new glass, then crawled onto the blanket next to him.

"Here's to tonight's most wonderful activities." In the last rays of evening light, his eyes were tender and warm. After a few seconds, Allie looked away as if the lake were a preferable view, afraid he'd see too much.

She couldn't imagine a preferable view.

"So, I have a manipulative great-grandmother, huh?" He leaned back on one hand, glass in the other, a perfect combination of virility and elegance. The guy had it all.

"Josephine knew what she wanted, and how to get it. Apparently there was a guy named Walter she'd decided to marry."

"She did."

"Really!" Allie was delighted. "I didn't get that far. Good for her."

"They had the five children."

"How did this property come down to you and Erik if there are that many relatives running around?"

"It's sad, actually. Two of mom's great-aunts and -uncles— Josephine's children—died, one in childhood, the other before marriage, so no kids there. One moved abroad and settled, and I think the other just wasn't interested. So it was just Grandma Bridget who hung on to Morningside. Mom was her only child."

"Wow. There's a lot of family history here. I don't see how you can chuck it."

"It won't be easy." He drained his glass, lay down and put a hand on her back. "Join me?"

"Sure." She dug her glass into the sand and lay down next to him, their hips, thighs and shoulders touching. He covered them with the second blanket.

"Not many stars out yet. We'll have to stay a while."

Allie grinned in the gathering darkness. "I guess so."

"Good, because there's a lot I want to know about you."

She stiffened. "Such as…"

"Erik said you grew up in Brooklyn."

"Yes." She felt the usual shame creep into her body. Talking about her childhood was an exercise in revisiting pain. So many people stuffed into such a small place, filthy and roach-ridden. The yelling. The drinking. Her father leaving for his rich girlfriend. Her brothers' subsequent anger and wild rebellion. Her mother's decline. The enormous responsibility Allie felt for keeping the family peaceful and afloat. The enormous determination she had to escape that life and never look back.

"What area? Park Slope?"

"Not far from there." Yeah, right. Only a world away. Park Slope had become trendy and expensive, salon blondes pushing designer strollers past sushi shops in neatly kept brownstones, lattes in hand. Nothing like her neighborhood in Kensington, where kids hung out on the stoops and yelled, jostled for control, for power, and harassed passersby. You had to have a pretty tough mouth and attitude.

Allie had learned to speak without an accent from TV, watching news and movies and squeaky-clean sitcoms. She might come from that neighborhood, but she wasn't going to look or act or sound as if she did.

"Where did you grow up?"

"Long Island. Town called Old Westbury."

Allie forced a laugh, freezing inside. She shouldn't be surprised, though Erik had never mentioned the town. Old Westbury was one of the wealthiest towns in the country. Vanderbilts and Du Ponts and Winthrops lived there…and Meyers apparently. Her father had taken her driving there once, pointing out the various immense estates, telling her not to settle for her mother's life, that he hadn't and that she shouldn't either.

"That bother you that I grew up there?"

"No, no, no." She was protesting too much. "Not at all. Must have been wonderful."

"My dad taught at the State University branch there, but yeah, Mom's family owned a house there, big enough for three families."

Three? Most houses she saw that day could have held twice that many. "Where did her family money come from?"

"Some early shipping magnate, we're talking colonial days. Then Josephine's husband, Walter, managed to save the family fortune from being lost to the Depression. Old Westbury is beautiful, but once I was old enough to realize life wasn't like that for everyone, it got uncomfortable pretty quickly."

"I can imagine." She couldn't. Not remotely. Once he realized life wasn't like that for everyone? How old had he been, twenty-five? Her upbringing would seem sordid and pitiable to him.

Allie took a deep breath in the dark. Or maybe it wouldn't. Projecting her own crap onto him wasn't fair. And yet, she was more convinced than ever that he'd never be able to comprehend her life any more than she could comprehend his. So why bother telling him?

"You said you have five brothers. Are you close to them?"

Allie twisted her lips, wondering how it would sound to say no. He and Erik had their differences, but they were obviously family in a way Allie and her brothers weren't, and probably never had been. "We don't hang out all the time. We have pretty different lives."

"Allie?"

"Mmm?"

"Why is this conversation making you so uncomfortable?"

His perceptiveness took her aback. With her last boyfriend, Raymond, she could have dumped gasoline on herself and been in the process of lighting a match, and he'd come into the room and ask if she'd seen his iPhone. "What makes you think I'm uncomfortable?"

"Your body is a brick wall."

"Oh." She sighed, moving restlessly, trying to relax. "Well, I don't know, really. My childhood wasn't that interesting. I'd rather hear about your career plans."

The waves gurgled in and sighed out; crickets sang hymns to the night; trees whispered their secrets to the breeze.

"Hmmm. Okay. My career plans. Those *really* aren't interesting. And they're only dreams at this point. But…let me think how best to describe it." His turn to fidget on the sand. "Workplace philosophies in this country are evolving and our company isn't. That's the sound-bite version."

"And you'd like to be able to help clients cope with the future instead of the present or past."

"Exactly. Let's say you're my client. My current company would examine this situation and say, hey, blanket, beach, darkness, very romantic, a good fit. However, as CEO of my new company, I'd say, okay, this is nice, but it could be better. Allie, why don't you try lying closer to Jonas so he can put his arm around you and really hold you?"

"Interesting recommendation." Ridiculously pleased, Allie moved closer and found herself enveloped comfortably in his arms, her head resting on his warm shoulder. "Wow. This *is* much better. You'll be a huge success."

"See? Now tell me, what would be your dream job?"

"Designing costumes for stage or screen. I majored in graphic design, because I figured well-paying jobs would be easier to find in that field. I did take some courses in apparel design, but in New York I'm competing against a bazillion people with full degrees."

"Ah, Allie." He sighed heavily. She could hear his heart thumping in his chest. "Maybe when we go home, we should both take a leap of faith. I keep telling myself to, but it's still not happening."

"Maybe we should." Except he had a safety net that could support a 747 falling out of the sky. She'd be an immediate splat on the pavement. "But right now I'm going to enjoy my time here with you and Josephine."

"You know, I was wondering…" He kissed the top of her head. "Are there any more good stories in that diary? Because I was thinking if you felt it very important to dress up and seduce me again, I would be glad to help."

"Oh, Jonas." She suppressed a giggle, sliding her hand to the center of his chest. "You are so sweet. Thank you. I might take you up on that."

"Yeah? When? Now? Middle of the night? First thing in the morning?"

This time she couldn't stifle her laughter. "Maybe tomorrow…"

"What time?"

She ran her hands down his chest, over his fly, then back up again. The awkwardness between them was forgotten now that talk had turned sexual again. She'd keep telling herself that was plenty until she believed it.

"You just leave everything up to Josephine and me."

CHAPTER EIGHT

"Now THIS—" Erik poured remarkably steadily from yet another bottle he'd excavated from the depths of his parents' liquor cabinet "—is a very fine tequila, the highest grade, extra *añejo,* which means—"

"Don't tell me, let me guess." Sandra held up her hand. She was enjoying Erik's company tonight much more than she'd expected to. Of course trying about ten different kinds of the highest-quality aperitifs, wines and liqueurs could make just about any situation pleasant. But aside from trying too hard to impress her, he was clearly intelligent and knowledgeable. She felt strangely at home with him in a way she never quite had with his brother. With Jonas she'd always been aware of the class difference that didn't really exist between them. "Extra aged."

Erik banged his hand on the kitchen counter between them. "Ten points for the woman in the sexy shorts and outrageously low-cut top!"

"Ding, ding, ding! Get her a prize!" She hoisted her glass to him, then let a small sip of the exquisite amber liquid past her lips. "Ooh. Nirvana in a glass."

"Don Julio Real. You're drinking about twelve bucks' worth right there."

"This?" She had about an ounce in her glass. "This itty bitty little drop?"

"It's not cheap." A beat later he realized she was playing him. "Hey, cut that out."

"What?" She blinked innocently, then dropped the act. "Nothing is cheap in this house and you know it."

"You hate that, don't you?" He swirled his glass, held it to the light, took a slow, careful sip and closed his eyes ecstatically. "Ah, *que magnífico!*"

"No, I don't hate that. I just don't always see the point." She took a larger swallow, strangely tempted to tell him the truth, that she'd grown up in a mega-mansion in Greens Farms, Connecticut, sullen and rebellious, loathing her parents' worship of the almighty dollar. And look at her now, kneeling at the same altar. "Except this stuff. If I had your money I'd buy this, too."

"Take a bottle with you when you go." He gestured to the glass-fronted cherry cabinet.

"Really?" She tipped her head. "So what, you're my sugar daddy now?"

"Sandra." He concentrated hard on her face. "You drive me crazy. I hope you know that."

"Sexually?"

"Sure. Sure." He nodded enthusiastically. "But also because I can't tell when you're kidding. It keeps me off balance."

"Ah." His admission surprised her. "You need to feel safe with a woman."

"I usually do." He winked at her. "But I don't need to right now. You're exciting."

"Well." Sandra lifted her chin, feeling a bit breathless. "Good to hear."

"Why, you want to excite me?"

"Absolutely. And for the record, I was kidding about you being my sugar daddy. If you want to spend money on me, all you have to do is…" She took a slow sip of tequila. "Marry me."

Erik laughed at that, as she hoped he would. A warm laugh. A nice one. She joined him because it felt so good to laugh with someone. And because she was starting to like him more and more, as she unearthed bits of him that were worth more than the rich guy who lived to get laid.

"Money is great, but the cliché is true, it don't buy happiness. Not the kind that lasts, anyway. I can get a high from a cool new toy, a new computer, a new phone, being the first to own brand-new technology. Or from a new woman, or a trip to somewhere I've never been. But when I get tired of the toy, the woman moves on or I return home, I'm back where I started." His features darkened. "That's what Allie was about. A shot at a life with real value—something lasting and important. I'm tired of being a rich playboy."

Sandra lifted a cynical eyebrow. "Then give it up."

"Not *that* tired."

"Right." She understood more than he knew. Easy to complain about money when you had plenty. "The gift you love to hate."

"I know. It's hard to understand when you're..." He stopped abruptly.

"Lower class?" She put her hand on his to stop his protest. "I do understand, Erik. But Allie isn't going to make your life perfect."

"I thought she'd be really good for me. I still do."

"How?"

"She's smart and interesting. She has depth. Plus she's classy and beautiful and isn't after my money."

"So wait." Sandra pretended confusion. "You don't want a woman with enough brains to value money?"

He guffawed at that, bringing to his face a boyish energy that was really appealing. She was developing a serious tipsy crush. "I like *you,* Sandra. You're smart. And practical."

"Ooh." She feigned dismay to hide her pleasure. "I've been called many things, but smart and practical? Not so much."

"You're sexy, too. I am insanely hot for you."

"And Allie?" Sandra pinned him with her best schoolteacher look. "Are you insanely hot for her?"

He glanced down at his glass. "She's a beautiful woman. I definitely want her."

"That's not what I asked, Erik."

"Okay." He met her eyes defiantly. "Yes, I am hot for her."

"Uh-huh."

He leaned forward until their faces were about six inches apart. His eyes were a really intense blue with long dark lashes, longer than his brother's. "Crazy hot for her."

"You know what's happening out there right now, with her and Jonas?"

Erik's face twisted. He drew back. "Yeah."

Sandra jabbed at him triumphantly with her index finger. "*That's* the only reason you think you're crazy hot for her right now."

"Not true."

She let that slide. They both knew it was. "Before this, have you ever wanted a woman who didn't want you?"

"No."

"But you wanted to marry this one." She paused to let him mull that over. "Did it ever occur to you that going after a woman who constantly rejects you keeps you safe from having to commit to this life you say you want?"

His eyes narrowed. He poured himself more tequila and topped off her glass. "Anyone ever tell you you're a major pain in the ass?"

"Only when I'm right."

"What about you? Still no tears over Jonas going at it with Allie?"

He was on the offensive now. Good to see. She'd get bored of a weak man. "None."

"Yeah? You weren't in love with him?"

"Nope." She took a bigger swallow than she needed. "Like him a lot, though."

"How about the men before him? Ever been in love?"

She narrowed her eyes. "What are you getting at?"

"Why aren't you married?"

"Don't want to be."

"How do you know *you're* not scared of it? Going after shallow relationships to keep from really falling?"

Sick anger burned through her, anger she was old enough to recognize as coming from his having hit a nerve dead-on. Little shit. He'd pay for that. She drained her tequila, got up, went around the counter to the sink, filled the glass with water and drank it empty, taking her time until she was calm again. "Let go of Allie, Erik. Your brother has her."

"It's preordained. Jonas gets everything. He always has."

His bitterness shocked her. She sat back down on the stool next to his. "What's that about?"

"Look at him." He flung an arm in the general direction of the cottage. "He's better-looking—"

"Debatable."

"More athletic."

"Possibly."

"Smarter."

"Could be."

"More successful."

"Definitely."

Erik scowled. "Feel free to disagree vehemently."

"Nuh-uh." Sandra waggled her finger at him. "That's not what you need from me."

He gave her a slow once-over that should have offended her, but didn't. "How do you know what I need from you, Sandra?"

"You'd be surprised." She started counting on her fingers, trying to forestall a blush. "According to you, your brother is better-looking, more of a jock, smarter and has a better job. Anything else?"

"Better relationships."

"Hmmm… What's next? No, wait, let me guess…he's your mom and dad's favorite."

Erik's eyes turned hurt. "How did you know that?"

"I didn't." She spoke gently, not wanting to make fun of him now. That pain she understood. "But it seemed a logical next on the list of grievances."

"You have any siblings?" He clutched his glass in both hands on the counter, his body close to her.

"Nope." She put a hand on his shoulder, surprised at the hard muscle underneath her fingers. "Honey, your list is not based on fact. It's all in your head. I wrote the book on crappy self-esteem. Took me a long time to get past it, and I still struggle. But it's worth doing. You have to love yourself in a healthy way before you can expect other people to."

"Pffft. New-age crap." He made the pronouncement mildly, more stubborn than sullen. She had the feeling he was listening.

"I bet you're thinking if Jonas gets Allie, it's another nail in your coffin of self-worth, huh?"

"Oh, jeez, put it in a psych textbook." He looked so much like a scowling kid getting a deserved scolding that she wanted to laugh. But she understood that kind of pain, too, so she wouldn't.

"It's not about Allie, Erik."

"No? What is it about?"

"You." Sandra put her hand on his thigh, a practiced sultry smile on her face. Bingo. Right where she wanted him. "Having a fun time up here after all."

Erik turned toward her, his eyes lit with sexual fire. He'd heard her. "Is this more flirting or serious?"

"Serious." She leaned toward him, breasts crowding each other in her tight turquoise top. "Take a good, long look and think about it."

"Look *and* think?" He gave his head a brief shake. "Can't do both."

She nearly spoiled her sultry pitch with a giggle. "There are rules, however."

"Rules."

"Yes. We're going to play a little game. One you've never played before."

"Okay." He hadn't taken his eyes off her breasts. Her nipples reacted to his gaze by coming wide-awake, which made him stare harder. She was amused…and turned on. The alcohol, probably.

"You're going to do something with me I'm betting you never did with any other woman."

"Oh." He took in a deep breath, blew it out, then met her eyes in that aggressive I-want-you way that made her have to steel herself not to back down. "I'll do it, whatever it is."

There went his deep feelings for Allie. First offer he got elsewhere, he jumped at. Gee, didn't every woman want to be loved like that?

"I'm only worried about one thing, Erik," she whispered.

"Yeah?"

"Yeah." She trailed her index finger across his mouth. A sexy mouth, slightly fuller than his brother's. "I'm afraid if you have me, I'll ruin every other woman for you."

He smiled his quick smile and chuckled. "I'll take that risk."

"Okay. Here it is." She leaned in to his ear. "We're not going to have sex until you open yourself to me. Emotionally."

He reared back to read her expression. *"What?"*

"Well?" She gestured triumphantly. "Have you ever done that with a woman?"

"I was *trying* to with Allie. It didn't work out."

"This will work out. But only if you tell me things about yourself. Big things, revealing things, secrets you've never told any of the women you've been with. Like feeling crappy next to Jonas. Each time you admit something deeply personal, you get a reward." Sandra brought his head down between her breasts. "This."

"Mmm." He nuzzled her, his touch and breath warm on her skin.

She slipped off the stool, took his hand and guided it around to her bottom. "And this."

His breath hissed in between his teeth. "Oh, yeah."

"And finally…this." She singled out his index finger, pressed it to the juncture of her thighs. Got him.

Except he freed his finger with ease, and firmly cupped her sex in his palm. Sandra froze for three endless seconds, feeling his fingers move gently. Unexpected arousal seared through her. She moved back abruptly, retrieved her booze glass from the sink and brought it back to him. "Hit me."

Erik looked at her uncomprehendingly, eyes still glazed. "You want me to *hit* you?"

"Erik, Erik, Erik." Sandra thumped her glass on the counter, annoyed with herself for coming so close to losing control of the situation. Guys like Erik were always in control. She'd be no different than any other woman if she fell apart under his touch. "Pour me more of something. Anything. Don't care if it's Marquis de La-dee-da or a wine cooler, as long as it has alcohol in it."

"Yes, right, okay." He got up from the stool, erection ballooning the front of his pants. There was something weirdly endearing about that messed-up kid. "How about Frapin Extra Grande Champagne Cognac, about $25 per ounce?"

Sandra rolled her eyes. "Blah-blah-blah, just pour."

He poured, grinning boyishly. "Not impressed?"

"Takes more than money to impress me."

"I'm beginning to get that." He held up his glass toward hers, inviting a clink. "I'm ready to accept your proposition. On one condition."

"What's that?"

"You have to tell me secrets, too."

"Of course." She clinked smugly. Her secrets were easy to tell. Her parents didn't want or love her, she married a much-older man who was a controlling jerk and she left him to become a stripper. She could tell the truth but leave out the pertinent details. Like growing up rich. Like being disinherited. Like the pain she carried around from being denied a real family by parents who treated her like the mistake she was, spending money on her when she wanted their time and affection. Like her brief foray into drugs, and the one night she'd come dangerously close to prostituting herself that officially counted as hitting bottom. Her battle to get clean and begin a new life supporting herself.

She'd bet a glass of Don Julio Real that Erik had never shared much with his hot young things besides bodily fluids. Feeling vulnerable to and validated by someone could be powerful stuff. And if things didn't work out between them and she failed to land his lovely lifestyle permanently, she'd still be teaching him to value women outside of a sexual capacity, a gift to her gender.

"When do we start?"

Sandra lifted her glass. "Another day. Tonight we just have fun."

"Okay." Erik grinned eagerly. "What kind of fun? Skinny-dipping? Naked Twister? Strip poker?"

Sandra sent him the exasperated look he was undoubtedly expecting. "This will be a new way of thinking about women, Erik."

"Oh, no." He looked distinctly ill. "We have to watch *Bridesmaids?* Play Monopoly? Alphabetize the CD collection?"

"All that and more." She laughed at his expression and tossed back her remaining twenty dollars' worth of brandy. "You're about to embark on the adventure of your life."

CHAPTER NINE

Dear Diary,
    Mum and Daddy went out tonight to a party at the Gullivers'. Such a pity! Because it meant Walter and I were alone. Well of course Dorothy and David were here, but I very generously gave them the night off and a few dollars to enjoy themselves with. Walter is very interested in Egyptian history, lucky for me. I asked him about it because I wore the most fabulous Cleopatra costume to a party last year, and it's been sitting around going to waste. The best part of the costume is the part no one ever saw, the undergarments. Walter will see those tonight. I'm thinking that one or two more nights of this should be sufficient. He leaves on the weekend. If I can get a proposal before he goes, I will count myself not only a successful seductress, but the luckiest girl in the country. He is a truly wonderful man, and my feelings are only growing stronger the more we talk.

Allie threw the Frisbee to Erik and managed a surreptitious glance at her watch. Was it broken? Ten minutes after the last time she'd checked it and only two minutes had passed. She was hoping for at least forty-five.

Her next "date" with Jonas would be in about an hour. Their little quartet had spent a quiet Sunday the day before, on the beach in the morning, then indoors during a rainy afternoon. Allie had passed the time in the attic. They had dinner together then watched a couple of movies—*P.S. I Love You* for the women and *Fight Club* for the guys. It had been late when the second movie finished, and Allie had been the first to announce that she was going to bed, followed by Sandra, while the guys looked forlornly after them.

Yes, Allie had wanted to be with Jonas, but she worried that spending every night with him would catapult them into what felt more like a relationship than a flirtation, and she wanted to make sure nothing serious developed. Already she was feeling too much.

Tonight, however, Erik and Sandra had plans to go into Glens Falls for dinner and to listen to music. Jonas had firmly declined the invitation for him and Allie, making it clear that Allie was not getting away from him. She grinned. Being desired was absolutely delicious.

The Frisbee came back to her. She caught it neatly and hurled it away. At least Erik was no longer flirting with her. He seemed to have switched quite happily to lusting after the sultry Sandra. Allie couldn't blame him, though she'd bet Sandra put up with a whole lot less of Erik's crap than most of the girls he dated. In any case, it meant that Allie and Erik could relax around each other, and their friendship had improved 100 percent.

Erik's next throw came at her too high, causing her to back up in a hurry, stumble on the sand, then make a stupendous jump... and miss. She ran after the Frisbee, wondering at this strange habit humans had of throwing things at each other. Balls, spinning plastic disks, boomerangs, batons...

"Sorry!" Erik called to her across the beach. "Don't know my own massive strength."

"Not as sorry as you're going to be." She retrieved the Frisbee and launched it back at him. He waited, gathered himself, made a leisurely leap and grabbed it. "Aww, lucky catch!"

She'd spent another hour in the attic today after she and Jonas got back from their hike and picnic lunch, unpacking yet another trunk of fabulous clothes—less fabulous than the ones she'd already opened, but still fabulous. The second round of trunks, one of Bridget's, one of Josephine's, held everyday dresses, some of which were timeless enough to wear now. There was also a wonderful array of handbags in gorgeous leathers, beads, velvets and satins, even one made out of ornately etched Lucite.

Then she'd dived into Josephine's diary again and come up with page twenty-seven and the corresponding Cleopatra lingerie outfit, a hilarious but sexy combination of a gold bandeau and black sequined panty with a tiny swatch of skirt in front and back. Completing the outfit were a black sequined cap, an ornate arm bracelet and gold chains for around her bared waist. On her feet she'd wear fabulously complicated strappy heeled sandals.

She might have kept Jonas at arm's length yesterday and today, but tonight they'd get very, very close.

"I'm done." Erik fell onto his towel, pretending to be exhausted. Sandra was upstairs taking a nap. Jonas had gone into town for groceries, then for another run. Allie had jogged with him earlier, but his stride was so much longer than hers that she doubted he'd gotten much of a workout and wasn't surprised when he said he was going out again.

"Yeah?" Allie lowered herself to her own towel, spread out next to Erik's. A few yards away, waves splashed in, the wake of a passing boat reaching them. Above them, cotton-ball puffs sailed past. So beautiful. "That's your workout for the day, huh?"

"For the week." He patted his slightly soft stomach. "I save my heavy exercise for the dinner table."

Allie snorted. "Nice."

"Allie, Allie, Allie."

"Ye-e-es?"

"You doing okay?"

She knew what he was asking. "Yeah. You?"

"I've been thinking."

"Don't strain yourself."

"Ha ha." He turned on his side and shaded his gaze from the sun. "You and Jonas are perfect for each other. Long term. Like forever."

"Uh…" Her insides burned with excitement, which annoyed the hell out of her. She didn't want to marry Jonas. But clearly her fantasies were running far ahead of reality.

"No, really, hear me out. You're classy. You grew up in a good family. You can deal with all this." He gestured around, indicating their property. "Not everyone is comfortable in our world. I don't blame them. It can be intimidating if you're not used to it. Money pisses a lot of people off. They struggle all their lives and never have enough, and here we are with so much and we never even had to lift a finger to get it."

Allie rolled her eyes behind her dark glasses. Oh, Erik. She'd never told him she grew up in a "good" family, whatever that was. He'd just assumed. Was she comfortable in his world? She pretended to be. She'd love to be. Maybe someday she could be. But he was right about one thing: he wouldn't be too comfortable in her mom's squalid three-bedroom apartment with five McDonald boys and however many girlfriends, all yelling at one another. Neither would Jonas.

When the Meyer boys had dinner with their parents, you could probably hear cells dividing.

She turned on her side toward him, anxious to change the subject. "*I* was thinking that you and *Sandra* are perfect for each other."

"What?" His lips curved in a smile, belying his outrage. "You can't be serious."

"She's a little wild, the way you are, but she fits here. She's taken this place totally in stride."

"She grew up in South Boston."

Allie groaned. "You say stuff like that, and I just want to smack you. Seriously, Erik, who cares? She's a class act, and you're a moron if you can't—"

"No, no, you're right. That slipped out. I didn't really mean it. See, you have to understand. Jonas and I were raised by snobs to be snobs. Neither of us really thinks money gives us value as people. But for our entire childhoods, this 'us versus them' philosophy was taught, by action if not words. It's hard to shake that off."

"I understand." She did. Because she'd learned, from her childhood and experiences with her father's snotty second family, that everyone with money looked down on those without. And her brothers never failed to point out that she should take pride in her poverty and stick to her own kind. Her aspirations for getting an education, dressing and speaking differently from her siblings, and making something better of herself earned her family's scorn and permanently damaged their relationship. There were snobs on all sides.

"Sandra isn't as perfect for me as you would have been, Allie. I need settling down."

"You?" She lifted her sunglasses to peer at him, wondering what he'd think about her level of wildness if he'd seen her seduce his brother. "You'd be miserable settled down."

"No, it's time. I'm thirty. I've been running wild too long."

"Well, then settle down with someone who can run wild the way you need to, Erik. Like *Sandra*."

Erik was quiet for a while, scooping sand and letting it trickle through his fingers. Had she reached him? "Maybe you're right. I need someone wilder than you. And you need someone steadier than me. Like *Jonas*."

"Nah." She kept her voice dismissive, annoyed with her racing heart. "We're just having fun. He lives in Boston, I live in New York—"

"Where you don't have a job. Perfect time to move." He snapped his fingers. "Hey, I can get ordained online and marry you guys."

"Erik!" She was laughing now in protest. "Enough."

"I'd *love* to have you as my sister-in-law," he said. "You could name your first child Erik. *And* your second."

Her phone rang. She dug it out of her beach bag, saving Erik from a mouthful of sand, and checked the display. Da Vinci Design! "Ooh, job phone call!"

He crossed fingers on both hands. "Good luck!"

"Hello?" Allie struggled to her feet, feeling silly taking a business call lying in the sand in a bathing suit top and shorts.

"Hello, Alison. This is Jennifer Birchfield from Da Vinci Design. I'm calling to tell you that we were impressed with your résumé and would like to have you in to talk about the assistant art director position."

Allie whirled to face Erik and pumped her fist. "Thank you, that would be great. I'm very interested."

Erik gave her a double thumbs-up.

"We're talking to people tomorrow. Can you come in at four?"

"Absolutely. See you then." Allie ended the call and let out a woo-hoo that Jennifer Birchfield could probably hear in the city.

"Interview?"

"Interview! Tomorrow! With Da Vinci! Assistant art director! I'm totally qualified. I have a good feeling about this."

"Do you have to leave tonight?" He looked crestfallen.

Allie's grin drooped and she felt a strange panic. No, she didn't have to leave that night, but she would have to leave early the next morning, depending on train or bus schedules. She wouldn't be able to get back until late tomorrow night. Or there might be a second interview she'd need to stay in the city for. Jonas was leaving Lake George first thing Wednesday morning.

Tonight could be their last night together.

JONAS LIT THE charcoal in the tiny grill on the cottage's back deck. You couldn't beat burgers on a hot summer evening. And these had a twist, with store-bought pesto mixed into the beef, and slices of tomato and fresh mozzarella waiting to top them. A burger *caprese* salad. He'd bought asparagus to grill, and of course, a bag of Lay's classic potato chips, his favorite. And watermelon.

On the counter sat a bottle of Bartolo Mascarello's 2008 Barbera d'Alba, a medium-bodied red that wouldn't be overwhelmed by the strong flavors in the burgers. A Duke Ellington album he'd bought on iTunes earlier that afternoon was playing on the iPod.

He was nervous, and not exactly sure why. He and Allie had had a nice day together yesterday and again today. After a run and swim that morning, they'd packed lunch and driven around to the east side of the lake for a short hike at Shelving Rock Falls, an easy three-and-a-half-mile round-trip, but a beautiful one, with spectacular views. He hadn't done that trail since he was a kid. Allie had seemed fairly relaxed, though he still had the feeling she was holding back, reluctant to open up about herself. Whether from fear or reticence, he wasn't sure.

Everything she did say seemed to come straight from her heart or her funny bone. Spending time with her made him realize too many of his interactions with friends and colleagues were superficial and serious. One of the reasons he enjoyed Sandra was how much she made him laugh. But apart from her, he'd somehow lost touch with the fun people in his life.

God forbid he turn into his father, obsessed with his studies, socializing only with other serious academics, attending parties with what seemed to be a permanent scowl. Dad had even been somber and intense about golf and tennis. Did he ever cut loose? Jonas couldn't imagine.

With Allie, Jonas was rediscovering—or maybe discovering for the first time—a more playful part of himself.

After the hike, Allie had retreated to the attic. Jonas had been restless, unable to sunbathe, read, nap or find anything to do that satisfied him. When he found out Erik and Sandra were taking off tonight, the idea of cooking dinner for Allie in the cottage came to him, and he'd jumped at the chance to shop for groceries. When that wasn't enough, he'd gone for another run, not very far, but fast. He'd needed to strain his muscles, to blow out some of this extra energy. He'd needed space to clear his head and try to figure out what the hell was going on.

It wasn't like him to be so unsettled.

Was it just that Allie had awakened the sexual beast that had been more or less dormant since Missy? In the last couple of days, since their erotic encounter on the deck, Allie had put distance between them, and he'd been nearly crazed with the desire to touch her, as much as he enjoyed her company on every other level. Maybe sexual frustration was building in him retroactively, from the long spell between partners, and he—

"Hello."

Jonas started, then turned sheepishly, embarrassment changing to ridiculous pleasure at the sight of her. Allie was dressed simply in a yellow and white vintage linen dress over some kind of gold camisole. Her wheat-colored hair was swept up and pinned at the back of her neck. Her tanned skin made her hazel eyes even more vivid. She looked sophisticated and elegant. His heart gave a painful thump. He wanted to kiss her. Badly. Instead he saluted her with the charcoal lighter as if it were a sword. "Hi."

"Sorry I startled you."

"No problem. I was pondering briquets."

"How deep." She looked over his blue shorts and casual white shirt in a hungry way that probably mirrored how Jonas had been looking at her.

Did he say he wanted to kiss her? Make that he really, *really* wanted to kiss her. Keeping himself from attacking her today had been physically painful.

But okay, he'd play it her way for now. They had two more nights this week before he left. He'd already decided to come up again next weekend so they could have two more. He could afford to be patient a while longer.

Then it would be his turn.

"Have fun in the attic this afternoon?"

"Ohhh, yes."

Just the way she said those two words made his cock stir. Plenty of women had turned him on, though he'd dated only two seriously, but none of them had engendered such a fierce, primal response from him. Allie wasn't the outwardly sexiest or most beautiful, but there was something about her that had pushed too many other thoughts out of his head, and made him want to alternately ravish and protect her.

Maybe she represented some fantasy come to life. Maybe he was secretly turned on by his great-grandmother....

Suppressing a snort of laughter, he led her over to the table on the deck where he'd set up the evening's beverages. "Glass of wine? Gin and tonic? First one then the other?"

"A gin and tonic would be perfect. Great summer drink."

"I agree." He plunked ice cubes into two tumblers, splashed in some gin and a squeeze of lime, and filled up the rest of the glass with tonic, wondering what she had planned for tonight and whether he'd survive waiting to find out. "Here you go."

"Thank you." She lifted her glass to his, her eyes dancing. "Here's to today."

"Today." He gestured her to sit. "Nice memories in that chair."

"So there are." She flashed him a sexy look and sat, crossing her thighs, reminding him of how she'd crossed her ankles so primly last time. Was this Allie more relaxed or a different character altogether? For a second he thought he saw something glint between her legs—he was a guy, of course he'd looked.

If she were any other woman, he'd be thinking glitter panties? What the hell?

But with Allie, he couldn't wait to find out.

"Jonas. It's truth-telling time."

"My truth or yours?" He sat in the chair next to hers, nodding when she pointed at him. "Okay. What do you want to know?"

"How many women you've had here."

"Had here like brought up to visit?"

"No, had like *had*."

"Hmm." Jonas put down his drink and pretended to count on his fingers, then switched hands, then switched back. "One."

"One?" She laughed in surprise. "No way."

"What did you expect?"

"I don't know. It seems like the perfect place for girlfriends."

"It does, doesn't it?" Part of him contracted into anger.

"But you never brought them here? How come?"

"My parents. Nice people, but very critical, controlling and very particular. Around them my friends were on eggshells, always afraid of doing the wrong thing." He smirked. "Erik was lucky, he didn't care."

"You did."

"Yeah." He stared moodily at the lake. "Some values and traits I'm glad and proud to have inherited. Others…"

"I think parents are put on earth to mortify all of us in front of our friends." She spoke bitterly, surprising him.

"Tell me—"

"But I want to know about this woman." She gulped from her drink. "The one you *had* here."

Her question derailed him. He'd wanted to ask her more about her parents, but she'd shut him down every other time he'd tried, too, so he let it go, though it bothered him she wasn't interested in sharing. It was another barrier she'd put up—one he was increasingly interested in breaching. "Ah, the woman. Practically a girl."

"You knew her a long time ago?" Allie wrinkled her nose. "Or recently and she was jailbait?"

Jonas held up his hand. "No, I was the young one, barely sixteen. She was wildly experienced, a couple of years older than me. I was sleeping alone in the cottage that night, and then suddenly I had company."

"Hmm." She grinned at him. "That sounds familiar."

"Mmm, yes, it does."

"So she just crawled in with you?"

"Sally. She was pretty wild. Had a rough life since then, I've heard."

"Oh." Allie tsk-tsked. "You ruined her."

"Must have." He got up and brought the bag of potato chips back to the table, along with a bowl of carrot sticks and sugar snap peas he'd found at the market. "Tell me about your first time."

She shook her head sorrowfully. "Awful. I'm surprised I ever did it again."

He lifted his glass to her. "May I just say how profoundly grateful I am that you decided to stay with the program."

She giggled and sipped more gin. She was emptying her drink faster than he was. Maybe he wasn't the only nervous one here tonight. The thought made him relax a little.

"Let's see. I was eighteen, first year of college, feeling very grown up and very independent, until a group of us girls got together one night to gab, and it turned out I was the only virgin."

"Or the only one admitting it."

"Wow." She looked up in surprise. "I bet you're right. I wish I'd thought of that then."

"So you decided to lose it immediately?"

"Uh-huh." Another sip, then she glanced at the level in the glass and put it on the table. "Let me tell you, there is no shortage of guys in college who'll help you out with that little problem."

"Ooh." He winced, immediately jealous of the undeserving jerk. "Tell me you didn't take out an ad online."

"Not quite. But…well, I could have chosen better."

"His first time, too?"

"I would hope so. Because anyone with that little clue after a decent amount of experience should just be taken out of circulation."

He cracked up. Allie had an extra edge to her tonight—maybe nerves, maybe not—but he was enjoying her even more than usual, and was thrilled she was actually talking about her past. "I'm truly sorry."

"Aw, that's okay. I learned my lesson." She sent him a wicked smile. "And went on to bigger and better things."

"Not touching that one." He got up, still too restless to sit still, and moved toward the grill. "I'm about to start cooking. How do you like your burgers?"

"Medium."

"Same." He spread the lit coals in the grill, put on the rack and closed the lid to let it heat. "Tell me what your dating life has been like since then. Serial boyfriends? Casual flings? Always someone in your life? Seldom? For one-night stands, press one. For serious boyfriends, press two. For—"

He loved the sound of her laughter, and the way she threw her head back and opened her mouth wide for the initial shout. Last time she'd come to him here, she'd been all cool sophistication and control. He liked her this way better. Around her he felt funny, sexy and, frankly, a little crazy. In a good way for the most part.

"I date when there's someone worth dating. There hasn't been lately. I had a serious boyfriend in college—as serious as you can be when you're too young to be serious. Then another one who broke up with me a couple of years ago. Nice guys, but…I don't know, not that exciting." She frowned, mouth bunching adorably, looking as though she was starting to feel the alcohol. "No, that makes me sound shallow. I'm not looking for nonstop thrills. Just…someone who accepts me as is. Wait, not that I wouldn't have to change anything ever, I mean that's impossible, obviously. But what I mean is—"

She broke off, looking bemused.

"You mean it's pretty much hopeless to explain why some relationships seem okay, but aren't."

"Yes." She looked at him as if he'd solved one of the primal mysteries of the earth. "I've worried it's me, that I'm too picky. Other times I think I just haven't met the right guy yet. I figure most people do find someone, so I should just be patient. And then I think, I drank three-quarters of my drink in about five minutes and my God I'm talking too much, I should probably eat something."

It was his turn to laugh, freely and without restraint. She surprised him. And delighted him, sober, tipsy, earnest, erotic, silly, he liked every side he'd seen of her.

And frankly would like to see a lot more.

"Your turn." She grabbed a carrot stick. "I have banned myself from talking. Tell me about your girlfriends."

"Okay. I've had two big ones."

"How big? Amazons?"

"Ha ha." He lifted the grill lid and used his scraper to clean the rack. "Two *serious* ones."

"They couldn't take a joke?"

"No talking, Allie."

She clapped her hand over her mouth and spread her fingers to speak. "Right, sorry."

"I dated around in college, but met Margaret after business school when I was working at Baldwin & Company."

"She worked there, too?"

"At the lunch counter. Art was her calling. Sculpture and multimedia. A great woman, lots of fun. Very strong. Very determined."

Allie made ape noises and mimed beating her chest.

"No more gin for you."

"I'll be good. Tell me more."

"At first I loved the challenge of her, but after a while she just exhausted me. Everything was a battle she had to win."

"Oof. No fun. Then who?"

"After Margaret, Missy. To be continued…" He went back into the house, brought out the burgers and put them on the grill to sizzle, loving the way Allie looked sitting on the deck, all yellow and white against the gray weathered boards, like a daffodil blooming on rock.

She caught him staring and smiled. "Missy?"

"Missy, yes. She turned out to be the opposite of Margaret, at least on the surface. Sweet, charming, with a high-level job. I wondered sometimes how she could manage people or money effectively by being so obliging. Then I discovered she was screwing a colleague and wanted me just for my money. Since then, there's been no one I've thought about seriously."

Until now.

The thought blindsided him.

"God, Jonas." Allie's expression turned to sympathy and, for a flash before it was gone, tenderness. She cared about him. At least some. "It's weird how we can be so blind to obvious destructive patterns when we start dating people."

"No kidding." He moved the burgers around on the grill for something to do while he got his thoughts back in order. Allie? He'd barely known her three days.

"It makes getting involved with someone sort of terrifying. My last boyfriend, Raymond, was a completely passive lump of a person." She waved her hand in front of her face, apparently dismissing Raymond's memory. "I was so thrilled that he adored me. I kept telling myself no one was perfect. I couldn't have everything in one man. And then, finally, I realized, well, no, Allie, but you should have *something* in him."

He felt that same tenderness he'd glimpsed in her eyes. He wanted to tell her she deserved everything, but didn't want to bring to her attention that she was finally sharing personal details. As it would be too much too soon coming from him. "When people are first dating they put on a show of being who they want to be, or who they think they are, rather than who they really are. So you waste all this time investing emotions into what is essentially fake."

Allie stiffened, made a noncommittal sound, picked up her drink and took another swallow.

Jonas flipped the burgers, wondering what he'd said. Nothing that applied to them. They weren't dating, just fooling around. Nor did he get the impression Allie was putting on any kind of a show. He certainly wasn't. So why had she abruptly put out the fire she'd brought to the conversation and to the evening?

He brought out the hamburger rolls and opened them, ready to warm them up. "Hungry, Allie?"

She came out of her trance and smiled. "You bet."

The hamburgers were delicious: juicy and flavorful, slathered with the pesto and topped with flavorful summer tomato slices and melting fresh mozzarella. Allie's eyes popped when she took her first bite and encountered the unexpected flavors, which pleased him way too much.

They chatted about the weather, their day, the area's history, her favorite places in New York, and his in Boston. The door into her life and the emotions had been slammed firmly shut.

After they ate, they brought their plates to the kitchen and sat outside, lingering over the bottle's last two glasses. Jonas didn't know when he'd felt such a crazy mix of contentment, anxiety and raging lust.

"I have watermelon. Would you like some?"

"Love some."

"Brandy?"

"Absolutely." Her skin was rosy in the evening light. Strands had come loose from her hairstyle and curled around her face in the lake air, making her look sexily mussed.

He got up, reluctant to leave her, even for a few minutes, and went into the kitchen, half-hard just from looking at her and imagining all the things he wanted them to do. At the counter, he cut a few slices of watermelon and put them on plates, then poured two glasses of the brandy he'd brought out from the house, put it all on a tray and carried it back to—

She was leaning against the railing, which she'd covered with beach towels so her body would be invisible from the lake, her back to him, staring out toward the water. He'd seen her in the pose before.

But not like this.

Her hair was covered in strips of black sequin-covered cloth— half wig, half hat—with a distinctly Cleopatra shape. A brass cobra coiled around her upper arm. The gold material he'd glimpsed under her shirt wasn't a camisole; it was a slender band covering her breasts. Below that, gold chains glittered around her slender waist. More black sequins stretched over her hips in a narrow band, extending into a tiny swatch of a skirt that barely covered her bottom. On her feet she wore black strappy sandals with medium-high heels. An Egyptian seductress.

She turned her head to reveal eyes lined with black, almond-shaped with a stripe extending from the outside corner almost to her hairline. Her profile caught the setting sun, the lake behind her, her body in beautiful silhouette. Exotic. Seductive.

He was no longer only half-hard.

Jonas put down the tray. "I'm not sure I'm still in the mood for watermelon."

"No."

"Cleopatra." He came up behind her, covering the delicate fingers resting on the railing with his hand. His chest pressed against her mostly naked back. His pelvis found black sequins, pushed suggestively against them. "Did anyone ever tell you that you have a great asp?"

A groan came out of her that made him work not to chuckle. He kissed her bare shoulders, one then the other, lightly bit her sweet-smelling skin, then soothed the bite with his mouth.

"Your servant is here, my queen," he murmured. "What do you desire?"

"Here." She tipped her head, leaving her long, graceful neck open for exploration. He happily complied, moving his hands to the narrow span of her waist, then following the chain around front to slip his fingertips over her stomach and under sequined elastic. Her skin was smooth, soft. He couldn't get enough with his fingers or his mouth.

"Very nice." His fingers returned to the small of her back; he stepped out of the way while they journeyed back under the sequins and around her firm bottom. Jonas closed his eyes, savoring her shape until his fingers grew impatient and pushed their way down and forward between her legs, where they encountered warm moisture…and cool air.

He stopped, puzzled. Was there a hole in—

Sweet heaven. Designed for easy access.

His turn to groan, as she had, but not for the same reason. He knelt behind her, lifted the small square of material and took his fill of the sight. Black sequins lined either side of her sex, her lush pink lips protruding from the neat gap in the fabric. Jonas pressed her legs farther apart, then counted slowly to three, letting her wonder what he was going to do, letting the breeze blow over her, making the light brown hair between her legs quiver.

Silently, he moved in. His tongue found her first. She gasped, her knees buckling before she recovered and leaned forward to give him better access. He tasted her greedily, steadying her hips with his hands. She was soft, sweet, her labia yielding and stretching under his tongue. A breeze blew around them, carrying the smell of the charcoal fire mixed with coming rain.

Eagerly he turned her toward him so he could find her clitoris with his lips, wanting her as hot and ready as he was. Wanting her to let go completely, to beg for his cock inside her. He wanted her to acknowledge in some way that she was as far gone as he was, that she could no longer fight the power of what lay between them. That what lay between them might be…important.

"Stop. Queen's…orders." She barely got the phrase out. "This isn't the plan."

"No more plan. Just you and me." He kept at her, using his lips to paint her, his tongue to thrust up inside, loving her taste, her smell, the promise of what they could do together tonight.

Without the costume.

He tried to ease the panties down, surprised when she grabbed them to keep them on. Okay. The gold band would go, then. He dragged it down around her waist so he could touch her breasts, admire their shape, taste the pink nipples that drew him to his feet.

She was gasping, her body trembling. "You're not— I was supposed to—"

He lifted his mouth from her breast, took her shoulders and pulled her close to kiss her fiercely.

She stiffened; her hands pushed weakly against his chest. He persisted, wanting her more than he'd ever wanted a woman, wanting to break through the barriers she put up, to get to the inner truth of her. He kissed her insistently, seductively, willing her to break, to show how much she wanted him back.

Finally she relaxed against him, parted her lips and wrapped her arms around his neck. Jonas's heart swelled with male triumph. He was going to take her right here, against the railing through the slit in her extraordinary panties. He retrieved a condom from his back pocket and shoved down his shorts and boxers with the same hand.

"What are you doing?" She spoke against his mouth with more alarm than he thought necessary.

"Condom."

"No. No sex."

He stopped kissing her, incredulous and angry. Another barrier? "What's up?"

"Sex is…not part of the—"

"So?" He snorted. "Because some ancient relative didn't, we can't? This is the twenty-first century."

"No, that has nothing to—"

"Is this part of some other manipulation, Allie? Because I'm not into power games."

"Stop. Jonas, calm down." She was clearly distressed. He ran his hand through his hair in frustration, taking a breath. Still on testosterone overload. He needed his brain to work here.

"Okay. Sorry. I should have just asked what the problem was. Is it some health issue?"

"No." She looked horrified. "I'm clean."

"Then *what?* You gave me every reason to think—" He tightened his lips. He was upset, but so was she. He needed to think about something more than the erection that would probably never go down. "Just talk to me, Allie. Tell me what's going on."

"I'm leaving tomorrow. I have a job interview in the afternoon."

"Okay." Luckily—since the testosterone-controlled part of him immediately wanted to ask what the hell that had to do with not having sex—his gentler side gained control of his speech. "That's great. What's the position?"

"Pretty much what I've been doing." She made a face. "But it's a good company. And it's a job."

He waited, stunned that they were having this discussion right now, hoping it was not due to more female logic he wouldn't understand. "Congratulations."

"So…I'll be back right before you leave. We'll barely see each other again."

He touched her face and smoothed her worried brow, vastly relieved. She didn't want just one night with him. He didn't want that, either. "I was already planning to come back up next weekend. We'll see each other again."

"Oh."

His relief faded, undone by her lack of enthusiasm. "That's a bad thing?"

"No. No." She pulled back, clearly exasperated. "I'm messing this up."

"Just say it. Whatever it is. You're not that interested, you're seeing someone, you're married, you're gay, you're into fish, you're into gay fish—"

"Stop!" She was giggling now, looking up at him through her Egyptian makeup, the black sequined headdress glittering. A wave of passion and tenderness swept over him. Yes, too much too soon, but he couldn't help himself.

He pulled off her headdress and dived his hands into her hair, loosening the pins, making them scatter. Her hair tumbled down and he brought her face to his. "We don't have to make love, Allie. But I want to understand. If it's not that we'd only have one night, what is it?"

"I just…" She inhaled and exhaled quickly, eyes down. "Panicked. I'm not Josephine. I'm…this is turning into something I didn't expect."

"Like…there's emotion involved?"

She folded her arms across her chest. "You think Cleopatra admits to that kind of vulnerability?"

"Hmm." A slow grin spread his mouth. "I don't want to feel anything for you, either."

"Well, good. That's two of us."

"So." He took her shoulders gently. "Now there's no problem. Neither of us wants to feel anything, so we just won't. It's all good."

"You—" she couldn't suppress another giggle, poking him accusingly in the chest "—are just trying to get back into my loincloth."

"I am *definitely* trying to get back into your loincloth."

She huffed in pretend outrage and turned her back on him. "This is why I surround myself with eunuchs."

Laughing, he wrapped his arms around her and held her close. Very close. His cock recognized heaven when it felt it and rose to attention. "Ah, but my darling Cleo, those eunuchs don't have—"

"I *know* what eunuchs don't have."

He laughed again, giddy and light, then kissed her shoulder as he had before, up her neck, to her jaw. She turned her head to meet his mouth, and their kisses, gentle and searching at first, became hotter, more passionate, until they were both breathless again.

"Allie…?"

"Yes," she whispered.

"No feelings involved."

"No feelings."

He rolled on the condom, pulled her hips gently toward him, applying pressure to her upper back so she bent forward. Then he reached around to make sure she was really ready for him.

"Oh," Allie whispered. She held still while he rubbed her clitoris. Then her head bent, her hips circled slightly and she whimpered. "That's good."

"Yes-s-s." He slid a finger inside her. She was tight and hot; he was starved for her. Two fingers. She squeezed him even tighter. "Do you like that?"

"Yes." She panted the answer. "More."

Somehow he kept from plunging into her to find his own relief. He kept his fingers working, exploring, stroking, lingering on her clitoris, and then backing off. Her gasps became louder. She flung her head back and gave a short cry, then another.

He gave in, spread her wide and thrust home, feeling her coming around him almost immediately. It didn't take much longer for him. Her muscles squeezing him, the sight of her sequin-clad ass swaying forward and back as he pumped her sent him shooting over the edge, no brakes, nothing holding him.

He came down gently, suddenly aware of the damp night and a few cooling drops of rain beginning to fall. He helped Allie stand, wrapped his arms around her and held her trembling body close, pressing his cheek to her temple, feeling his heartbeat gradually slowing, watching the rain coming toward them across the lake, aware of her warmth and her fresh scent.

And he suddenly understood why Allie hadn't wanted to make love tonight. And why he'd been so restless and nervous today.

No feelings? Ha. More like nothing but feelings. She was right to be afraid. This was supposed to be a hot fling: a fun and sexy chance for Allie to act out some fantasies and for him to escape his normal life, which lately seemed to be channeling him into the sort of narrow, uncreative existence he'd always dreaded.

But his feelings for Allie had evolved to where avoiding the pain of losing her felt like a life-or-death situation.

Jonas closed his eyes, chuckling silently without humor.

For the first time, he was beginning to understand Erik.

CHAPTER TEN

"WHAT IS THE appropriate after-dinner drink for revealing secrets?" Erik stood outside his parents' cabinet, which held more bottles than Sandra's liquor store. "Ever tried Italian amaro?"

Sandra shook her head, tipsy after one too many Tsingtao beers with dinner. Or maybe two too many. "No, but I've heard it's when the moon hits your eye like a big pizza pie."

"'That's amore.' And we are both way too funny."

"True."

They'd just finished a meal of takeout Chinese, which Erik had ordered from his favorite place in Glens Falls—not bad, even a city snob like her had to admit. Now they were approaching the second part of the evening, when Sandra's plan was being put into effect.

She was weirdly anxious, not quite able to get her bearings. Thinking alcohol might relax her, she'd overindulged.

It hadn't worked. And she was very annoyed, with herself and with the circumstances. This evening should be easy and pure fun. Erik would confess something that mattered to him, she'd hear it, tell him something that didn't particularly matter to her, and then they'd make out.

Not exactly earthshaking. Not exactly life-changing. So why couldn't she escape the feeling that she was somehow in up to her neck?

Allie had left that morning for her interview in New York. Jonas had left to go back to Boston soon after. He'd be taking his vacation day another time—when Allie was free to join him. They seemed right together, and she was happy for Jonas. Her jealousy had completely subsided, partly because Erik...well, Erik was fun. Really fun. Jonas had been fun in a more subdued way. She felt safe with him, knowing she could depend on him for anything, that he was a rock-solid kind of guy. Eventually she might have gotten bored.

But Erik was exciting. A bit dangerous. Not because he had a cruel bone in his body from what she could tell, more puppy than pit bull, but because if they made any kind of committed relationship out of this, she'd have to work to keep him. That uncertainty would make some women crazy, but Sandra was pretty sure she needed that excitement to stay interested herself.

Her husband, Edwin, had been controlling, jealous and obsessed with her. Jake, her boyfriend after that, had been the same. Erik seemed to accept her and her sexuality as thrilling, not threatening. They were turning out to have a lot in common.

"This is Amaro CioCiaro, an orange-flavored liqueur, slightly bitter." He pulled out the cork and poured two generous measures into tiny curving glasses that looked as though they'd shatter if you sneezed on them. "Amaro means 'bitter' in Italian. But because it's a liqueur, the bitterness is balanced by a sweetness."

"Sounds delicious, Professor Boozy."

"It is." He handed her a glass, his eyes warm. "And so are you."

"Well, thank you." She knew better than to melt under what was probably reflex charm, but it was a nice compliment. She'd worn a red clingy top that wasn't particularly revealing, but she knew the shade set off her dark coloring well. "You're looking quite edible yourself."

He was wearing a blue-and-white Indonesian print shirt, cheerful and summery but of course in exquisite taste, over khaki shorts. His arms and legs were muscular, as if he worked on his body more than his casual I'm-so-lazy attitude would lead one to think.

She sipped the drink, finding it intensely flavored, a fascinating combination of bitter and sweet.

"Like it?"

"I do." She walked up to him and put a hand on his chest, her suspicions confirmed by well-shaped pectoral muscles. "Hey, what's this? I'm thinking gym membership."

He blinked, in the middle of a sip of amaro, and then recovered. "You are, huh?"

"Am I right?"

"If I say yes, does that count as telling you a secret?"

"Not in a million years."

"Yes." He took her hand and led her out on the house's screened-in porch, where he seated her on an upholstered bench swing and plunked down next to her. Close.

So. They'd start now. She was still a bit…off, and she couldn't quite figure out why, but over her lifetime she'd become an expert at faking confidence she didn't feel. Came in handy quite often, actually.

"Well, Erik." She lifted her legs and swung them across his lap, arranging herself comfortably against the side cushion on the swing. "Tell me everything."

"Okay, then. Everything coming up." He took another sip, put his glass down and laid his hands on her bare shins, caressing them up and down, almost absently. "Starting with tonight's secret, Secret Number One."

"I'm ready."

"When I was a young teenager, I was bored here. My parents were pretty strict. Jonas hung out with a few kids close to his age, mostly older. I was the little brother they didn't want around."

"Ouch." She could picture him, maybe a little chubby, hiding his hurt at being left out.

"Aw, it was just basic kid stuff." He picked up her leg and started a gentle massage of the muscles in her calf. "But I was lonely and pissed off about it. There was a general store not too far from here, about a mile down the road, where the gas station and convenience store are now. It was old-school. You could buy nonperishable groceries, raincoats, fishing gear, hardware items, a few toys, stuff like that. There was a great assortment of candy up in the front next to the register, and behind it were shelves with magazines and personal pharmacy stuff.

"The owner had a son about my age. I hated this kid for no reason except he was skinny and weird-looking and had to spend his summer working in his father's store."

"Perfect anger target for that summer."

"A couple of summers." He shook his head, picked up her other leg and continued his massage.

"Hey, Erik?" She trailed her fingers down his arm. "Can I hire you to come home with me and do that every night?"

He gave her a slow smile. "Absolutely."

"Good." She waved at him to continue before she started going soft on him. "Now go on."

"What, that's not enough? My hidden hatred for the poor blameless angel of a child?"

"Nope." She folded her arms across her chest and regarded him sternly. "There's got to be serious dirt dug up here."

"There will be." His fingers stopped massaging and lay still. She had a feeling he didn't realize how hard he was squeezing her leg. "I figured out that at lunchtime the kid was in there alone. Alan, his name was. I'd ride my bike over whenever I could get away. Must have been a couple times a week. I'd wait until he was with a customer somewhere in the store, or I'd ask him about something behind the shelf. Then I'd steal candy."

"Oh, the ultimate irony—a rich-kid shoplifter."

He nodded, looking adorably contrite. "It gets worse."

"Mmm, goody."

He relaxed his grip, bent her leg and began massaging her foot. She closed her eyes and groaned in pleasure. Immediately, the massage stopped. Sandra opened her eyes to find Erik looking at her with such feral intensity she nearly gasped.

"Damn it, Sandra, you are so hot, sometimes it's all I can do not to attack you. I've never felt this way about anyone."

For a second, she sat there stunned by the passion in his out-burst.

That makes two of us.

"Well." She tried for a cocky unconcerned tone and failed utterly, struggled to sit up higher, as if her position had inter-fered with her voice. "You know what you have to do to make that possible."

"Yes." He turned back to her foot, leaving her somewhat shell-shocked. How many men had told her they wanted her? Dozens. She was well aware of the vibe she put out, but she also knew how to handle herself and had always felt well in control of the men and of her own actions and emotions. Not so much now. She didn't like it.

"Keep talking."

"This went on for two summers. Then I grew up some and realized Alan's dad was probably just making it financially and that I'd been a complete shit."

"No argument there."

"The next summer, the store wasn't there anymore. I was probably fifteen, sixteen by then. So I did some digging and found out where this kid lived, so I could give him and his dad back the money for what I stole. And then some."

"Ooh, noble child." She was more caught up in the idea of the struggling teenage Erik than she wanted to admit. "What happened?"

"I went to his house, in this sort of run-down neighborhood. Their place wasn't so great, either. I was about to go up and knock, when the kid came out. He had a girl with him, she was pretty, and they were laughing. Then his dad came out and told them to go have a great time, he passed his kid some cash and they headed for a car at the curb not far from where I was standing with a bunch of twenties in my pocket."

"And…?"

Erik turned and sent her a look of world-weary amusement. "And I turned chickenshit and went home."

"Oh, no!" Sandra nearly choked on her last sip of amaro. She put the glass down. "No, no, that's not how it goes. You give them the money and then the kid says, 'Oh, this is the exact amount I still need for the life-saving operation on my darling mama.'"

"Nope. I chickened out."

"So, then." She beckoned, prompting the rest of the story. "Years later, you found him again and sent an anonymous check?"

"Nope."

"At least tell me you've felt guilty all these years."

He looked pensive. "Not really. It was probably twenty-five bucks' worth. They survived."

She threw up her hands. "Not even penitent!"

"He became a corporate lawyer and probably bilked hundreds of people out of much more than I ever did."

"Erik! That's not the point."

He laughed, squeezing her bare foot, lifting it to his lips for a kiss. "I'm kidding, my darling Sandra, though he did become a successful lawyer. I did go back to his house, and I did my penance. I told Alan I'd been stealing from the store. He got this look of disdain on his face. I'll never forget it. Then it got worse."

"Oh, no." She was past being flip, genuinely caring about what happened.

"Because then he said, 'I know. We had a mirror behind the counter. Every day I put back whatever you stole from my own pay.' I was flabbergasted. So I asked the kid why the hell he'd cover for me. He said his dad didn't need any more stress. That the last jerk rich kid they accused got off clean and then his parents sued the kid's father. He said he would have gotten together boys his age to beat the crap out of me but his religion prohibited that kind of violence."

"Argh!" Sandra clutched her chest. "Drive a blade through your heart."

"No kidding." Erik's voice was choked. "I never felt like such a jerk in my life. I'd like to say it changed me. It should have…I don't know, made me see the world in a different light or something. You know, how it works on TV."

"Hey." His honesty touched her. She knew what it was like to want to change and not be able to. "We're all a lot more complicated than that, Erik."

"True."

"And I bet you never stole again."

"No."

"So that was something."

He nodded and drained his drink as if the emotional effort had cost him, probably not realizing it had cost her, too. "You want some more?"

"No. Thanks."

"Okay." He put his empty glass under the swing, then straightened and patted her on the knee. "Now it's your turn."

She changed positions, wondering how to start, how to tell. Decided to blurt it out and get it over with. "I'm not as good a storyteller as you are. My secret is that my parents didn't want children. And they never really bothered to hide that I was a mistake and a massive inconvenience to them." She laughed uneasily. "Sordid, but there you are."

Erik narrowed his eyes. "That doesn't count."

"What?" She blinked at him. "Why not?"

"Because you just said it, as if you were telling me what you had for lunch."

Sandra bristled. "What, I'm supposed to bleed all over?"

"Yes. That's what makes it a secret."

"*I* made the rules of this game." She was suddenly furious and went to pull her legs off his lap. He held them there with strength she couldn't fight.

"My little unloved girl."

"Not yours."

"Not yet."

"Not ever."

"Is this why you aren't married? Because your parents didn't want you so you assume no one does?"

Her mouth dropped; her throat thickened. She tried to get up off the swing, but he wouldn't let her move. "You don't know anything about me."

"Because you won't let anyone know you. Because you're afraid if someone saw you as you really are, they'd run, not love you, is that right?"

Her breath was too shallow, tears rising too quickly to stop. Damn it. This game they were playing was supposed to go the other way. She wasn't supposed to have to reveal anything.

"Leave me alone. You don't know me."

"Actually, I think you and I are remarkably alike, Sandra."

"You are remarkably full of sh—"

His kiss was hard, passionate, cutting off her words, setting the swing in motion as he lunged over her. Her sexual response was fierce and quick, but as quickly as it started, the kiss was over, and Erik was back seated on the swing.

She stared at him, still panting, but with the fight-or-flight slowly draining out of her.

If he'd seemed triumphant or the least bit smug, she would have punched him in the nose. But his eyes were serious, his forehead lined with concern. "You okay now?"

"Yes." She swung her legs down and tucked her hands under her thighs. He'd kissed her the way you'd slap a hysterical person. She didn't know whether to feel protected or violated.

Erik stopped the motion of the swing. "So."

"So?" She barely glanced at him. Every emotion she'd experienced still swirled through her. Anger, shame, grief, fear and a tiny bit of something vulnerable and sweet, as if Erik had reached a place she was only dimly aware she had.

"Are we done?"

"Yes." She knew what he wanted. She'd promised him access to her breasts if he told her a secret. The idea of him cashing in on their deal sickened her as much as it excited her.

"Want to take a walk?"

Sandra looked at him in surprise. "A walk?"

"Yeah. Along the lake. It's nice this time of night. No black flies. Too breezy for mosquitoes. Want to go?"

Why? He'd earned the right to touch her. A deal was a deal, and she had not ever weaseled out of a promise in her life.

"What about... You told me your secret."

"Jeez, what kind of guys have you been hanging out with?" He didn't try to hide his distaste, got up off the swing and held out his hand. "Give me more credit than that. You think I'm going to put you through an emotional wringer and then say, 'Okay, done, can I play with your tits now?'"

She giggled and gave him her hand, feeling lighter, younger, definitely relieved. "I guess when you put it like that..."

"We'll go for a nice walk, we'll have a good time, come back all relaxed." He held the screen door open and followed her down the steps. "And *then* I'll play with—"

"Do *not* finish that sentence."

He laughed and put his arm around her, pulled her close. "I really like you, Sandra. Want to move to New York?"

"Not in this lifetime."

"I could get used to having you around."

His words pleased her absurdly. But not, as they were supposed to, simply because they meant she was succeeding at reeling him in. They pleased her because it was really pleasant to be liked. Really pleasant to be with him out here on a beautiful night.

They walked until the sand ended and the rocky shore began, swinging hands, letting their bare feet swish through the water's edge. Then they turned and retraced the journey, passing the house, meandering along the beach until rock reclaimed the shoreline again on the other side of the property.

Back at the house, they returned to their seats on the swing with big glasses of ice water, chatting some, but already comfortable with silences.

Sandra hadn't felt so at peace, so content with a man...ever. Maybe with some of her gay friends in the theater. But even they were always wanting to talk, to share themselves. She'd always wondered why people seemed to open up to her so easily. Maybe Erik was right, maybe they came to her because she didn't tell them anything in return, didn't burden them back with a need for opinion or advice.

They talked on, until the moon was high and Sandra was tired of talking. She put down her water and pulled her top up. And off.

Erik stopped talking.

She folded the shirt, took off her bra, folded it neatly, too, and carefully tossed the clothes onto the chair next to the swing.

Then she sat, letting the swing rock, one arm along the back of the cushion behind them, the other on the side.

"Sandra." His voice was husky in the near darkness.

"Yes, Erik?"

"You are beautiful."

His touch when it came was not carnal, not greedy, but reverent, gentle. She hid her climbing arousal, kept her body relaxed, and he controlled his, keeping his movements slow, unhurried. Gradually she got used to the steady simmer of desire and let herself sink into the sensations. His hands were smooth and capable, testing the weight of each breast, moving over them in leisurely caresses. His mouth found her nipples one at a time, sucking and exploring with firm lips, swirling warm patterns with his tongue.

Only once did she betray her reaction, when her breath caught as his teeth gently grazed her areola. Then gradually the sweetness became confused with too much lust, and she turned the corner from wanting power over him to wanting *him*. But just as she opened her mouth to surrender, to tell him he could give it to her any way he wanted, he stopped, lifted his head, and kissed her gently.

"Thank you, Sandra. You are an amazing woman."

"You're welcome." She sounded as dazed as she felt, already missing his touch. Not since grade school had a guy stopped after petting, and back then it was because she made him. Erik could have done whatever he wanted.

"Ready for sleep?" He stood, solidly masculine, holding out his hand to her as he had earlier that evening, the consummate gentleman, except for the erection pushing out his shorts.

Ready for sleep. Not ready for bed. He was honoring her rules. Sandra didn't want honorable. She wanted sex.

Giving him her hand, she let him pull her up and lead her inside and to the second floor. She was supposed to be guiding this. She was supposed to be doling out the sexual favors one by one, and here he was leaving her in a state of such violent arousal, she was going to have to bring herself off in bed.

"Good night." He pulled her to him and kissed her. Once. A nice, sweet good-night. Twice. Longer, his mouth lingering. The third time she responded, pressing her body against his. A second later, she found herself backed against the wall, his erection pressing into her, his eyes glazing with lust.

"Good night, Erik." She managed a smile and slid out from under him, headed down the hall to her room, knowing he was watching. But instead of feeling triumphantly back in control, she felt dirty, ashamed of the cheap bait-and-switch she'd pulled on an honorable guy.

In her room, she collapsed onto the bed, badly shaken. In one day Erik had changed from the guy she had to teach a lesson to, into someone she had to defend herself against or…

Or what?

She didn't know. All she knew was that for the first time in many years, she was in a position she swore up and down she never would be again.

Way over her head in a situation she herself had instigated.

CHAPTER ELEVEN

"So you're getting a second interview—that's great."

"Yes." Allie nodded several times to make up for the lack of energy in her voice. "They seemed really excited about me."

Julie flicked her a glance. She was standing in front of the full-length mirror on her bedroom door, wearing skintight black pants and a belted tunic, clothes strewn over every available surface except the bed space Allie occupied. Tonight Julie was going out Wednesday-night clubbing with her boyfriend, David, and friends from work at Condé Nast. Apparently none of the gazillion outfits she'd tried on already made the correct fashion statement. "I'm sure they're excited about you. But you don't seem that excited about them."

"No, no, I am. I need a job. They have one I can do. It's perfect."

"Oh whee, that sounds thrilling." Julie yanked off the belt and tunic. "I give up on these pants. Nothing looks right with them."

Uh…tight black pants on a tall, model-perfect body like hers? Everything looked right with them. Allie had given up on suggestions half an hour before. Julie certainly had strong ideas about how she didn't want to look. Eventually she'd stumble over how she did. "It *is* thrilling. My long weeks of unemployment could be just about over, and I might not starve. That's cause for celebration."

"When are you going back to Lake George?" Julie turned to her dresser and started rummaging in her bottom drawer.

At the mention of the lake, Allie felt an immediate stab of misery. "I thought I'd rent a van and go tomorrow, early. Just pick up the clothes and come back the same day."

"What? You're not staying up there?" Julie straightened, holding a black camisole with a glittering floral design. "But Jonas will be there for the weekend."

"I know, I know." Allie flopped over onto her back and glared at the ceiling. She'd been having this battle with herself for the past two days. "I just don't see the point of going back there, falling for him harder and then saying goodbye. I don't want to date someone I see once a month."

"He's loaded. You could probably see him every weekend."

Allie lifted her head. "Once a week? Would that be enough for you?"

"If I could see us working out long-term, I'd at least try it. What about this?" She turned to Allie in the camisole, arms spread.

"Well, I can't see us working out long-term." She eyed her friend critically, her brain coming up with her own fashion ideas. "It looks great. Like everything else you've tried on."

"Why won't you and he work out?" Julie demanded.

"We just wouldn't. We're too different." Allie rolled off the bed and grabbed paper and a pencil from Julie's desk. "I wish I had those clothes here now for you. There was this fabulous shirt, black with lace sleeves and two lace panels over the boobs, lined with skin-colored fabric, that was both sexy and elegant. No one is wearing stuff like that now. You'd look incredible in it, with a little fascinator in your hair and a narrow skirt or wide pants. Something like this."

She finished the sketch with a few bold strokes and handed the paper to Julie.

"Yes!" Julie smacked the paper decisively. "*That's* what I want. Can you make it for me in half an hour?"

"Uh…"

"Seriously, that would be the perfect look." Julie gazed rapturously at the drawing, and then lifted her head to glare at Allie, jamming her hands on her hips. "You are an idiot not to be pursuing fashion design as a career."

Allie snorted. "Yeah, thanks, but I'd like to make enough to live on."

"So…" Julie dragged off the camisole. "Marry Jonas and you won't have to worry."

An undeniable thrill shot through her. Security, safety, for the rest of her life…

Allie recoiled from the bottom of her soul. What was she thinking? "Come on, that sexist crap is so not me!"

"Why not? If you're crazy about him anyway, and he's crazy about you, which it sounds like he is." She glanced at her watch, cringed and bent back to her drawer.

"We just met! I can't even *think*—"

"I *know* you just met. I'm not suggesting you propose tomorrow. But if things work out, since he's got craploads of money, he could support you while you—"

"No." The word exploded out. "I am not letting any *rich* guy support me."

Julie gave up on the drawer and turned back to her closet, totally unfazed by Allie's outburst. "Wouldn't you be happy to support him if your roles were reversed and *he* wanted to start a new business?"

"Well, yeah, I guess so. But that's different."

"Now who's being sexist?" She pulled out a black top that looked as if someone had slashed it into ribbons, and paired it with a red skirt still on the hanger. "And how are you and Jonas so different? It sounded as if you got along great."

"He grew up in Old Westbury, and I grew up in Kensington."

Julie looked up with an incredulous stare. "Uh, Allie? You need to figure out what the real issue is, because that is just plain stupid."

Allie dropped her eyes, calming her temper before she responded. Maybe it was stupid to Julie, and maybe it was true that Jonas wouldn't care, but Allie did. And her caring this much, right or wrong, meant it *was* a real issue. "Our lives have been so different, it's like we can't connect. We're fine flirting, fine chatting, but when it comes to real sharing…"

"Okay." The black pants were off and flung onto an already-loaded chair. Julie stepped into the red skirt. "So how did he react when you told him how you grew up?"

"I didn't tell him."

"What? Why not?" She zipped up the skirt. "I forgot about this skirt. I like it."

Allie peered over the side of the bed. "Didn't you wear that on your date with Kendall the night he—"

"Stop!" Julie held up a hand, turning side to side in front of the mirror. "Not another word about that creep. This skirt is the only one I've tried on today that might work, and if I think about him I won't want to wear it. So why didn't you tell Jonas?"

"Because it wasn't the right time. We were having a great, fun fantasy time together." Allie sighed. Julie would never understand. "Why bring my ugly reality into it?"

"You know, the only person who really can't handle your childhood circumstances is you. I bet Jonas would be fine." She'd struggled out of the black shirt, having gotten herself hopelessly tangled in the slashed ribbons. "Damn it. Now I remember why I never wear this thing. Can you help?"

"Sure." Allie took the top and started following the fabric strips from the side and shoulder seams, trying to figure out what belonged where, and where Julie's head and arms fit. "I do see your point. But I think I made the right decision."

"*I* think you're using something that hasn't been a factor in your life for over ten years to keep people from getting close to you."

"I do not mind getting close to people." Her temper rose again. "Hold your arms still."

"To keep men away, then. And don't bring up that Raymond story. He was a jerk."

"He was, but case in point." Allie had been crazy about Raymond at the time—of course hindsight was twenty-twenty—and things had been going well between them for nearly a year. Then he'd come to her mom's apartment to meet the family. Her brothers had gotten into a huge argument, her mom drank a whole bottle of wine after three cocktails and insulted Raymond's taste in food and music, and a cockroach had run across the kitchen floor while they were washing up. Things went from special to splitsville within two weeks.

"*I* love your family."

"When you come over, my brothers can't talk because they're drooling too much." She moved the last strip of fabric to the right place and pulled the shirt back over Julie's head. "Ooh, we have a winner!"

Julie turned to the mirror and smiled. "I'd rather have what you'd designed, but yeah, okay, this will do."

"You look fabulous. Have a great time tonight."

"Do me a favor." Julie caught her arm as she passed her. "No, two favors."

Allie rolled her eyes. "Uh-oh."

"One, stop trash-talking your family. The only person who comes out looking trashy is you. Two. Think seriously about taking this job you're not really excited about. Life is too short to piss it away on things that don't really matter to you."

Allie clenched her teeth. Easy for Trust Fund Julie to say. "I get that, but—"

"Think about it." She gave Allie's arm a shake. "Just think seriously about it."

"*Okay,* okay. I'll think seriously." She met Julie's eyes and softened her voice. Her friend was worried about her and trying to help. "I promise."

"And two…"

"No, you already did two. I'm done."

"Not done, now there's three. Three." She pulled Allie closer. "There is something about the way you react to this guy Jonas that you need to figure out. Because I believe with every fiber of my being that if you do, you will unlock some crap about yourself that you desperately need to be rid of in order to be happy. So my number two is—"

"Number three."

"Number *three,* then." She got right in Allie's face. "Promise me, *promise me,* you will go back up to Lake George and see Jonas again this weekend."

JONAS TURNED OFF Lake Shore Drive into Morningside's driveway. His tires spun briefly, throwing up a shower of gravel. He was going too fast, but he was pissed off and more than ready to be back. The drive had been brutal, the MassPike bumper to bumper with Friday summer traffic, slowed further by not one, but two accidents. Any sane person would have waited to drive up early Saturday morning. But he was apparently not sane.

Now, instead of arriving in time for a leisurely afternoon with Allie to start their weekend together, he was here at nearly dinnertime, while Allie had apparently tried to rent a truck—why the hell hadn't Erik made it clear they'd ship the trunks to her at their expense?—and then waited hours at the office only to find the truck had broken down and wasn't going to be available. Now she was on a bus and had hit Friday traffic, too.

He pulled in next to Erik's car, quashing the foolish hope that Allie would miraculously be waiting for him, outfitted in the latest 1920s erotic attire. Or better yet, in nothing.

As if on cue, his phone chimed the arrival of a text from Allie.

Still barely moving. Should arrive around seven maybe?

Seven. Two more hours. He could have gone to his morning client meeting instead of rescheduling. His boss had not been happy with the cancellation, or with Jonas taking more time off while they were at a crucial phase of developing a new client.

Jonas didn't really care.

As long as he was in the process of making lists of everything pissing him off, he'd add that not caring bothered him, too. Jonas had always cared about doing a good job, even if the work didn't thrill him. Not just at this job, at all of them, starting with his bakery job as a teenager. Did it matter if flour under the ovens wasn't swept up since no one would see it? Maybe not. But even though the other employees his age sneered at him, he wanted to be better than just adequate. *Do your best work or don't bother* had been his dad's mantra. Jonas had always done his best. *Erik* was the one always trying to get away with less.

Out of the car, he paused for the first long breath of clear lake air, feeling a reluctant sense of homecoming. They'd need to put the house on the market soon, maybe before the end of summer while people were still thinking about the season. They'd have to hire a real-estate agent, make sure the house was in good shape, decide about storing the contents, all while communicating overseas with his parents for instructions and signatures.

Giant pain in the ass.

In the cottage, he hauled his suitcase up to the bedroom, running his hand over the freshly made bed—Clarissa would have been there that morning to clean and change sheets. He hoped to be sleeping in that bed with Allie tonight.

The thought brought on a burst of pleasure and a dark burn of irritation. Or was it fear? He didn't know what the hell was happening to him anymore. After an emotionally charged goodbye on Tuesday, she'd returned to New York and to an emotional arm's length for the rest of the week. Until yesterday, he hadn't even been sure she'd be back this weekend.

But he was absolutely sure he wanted to spend tonight with her, feeling her naked body against his all night long.

Unpacked, he headed downstairs and out toward the big house to see what Erik was up to and find out how things had gone with Sandra this week. She'd probably passed Jonas on the highway heading back to Boston for weekend performances—going sixty-five, while he was lucky to go one-quarter that fast.

"Erik?" He pushed open the door.

"Hey, Jonas. In here."

Jonas strode toward the kitchen, and stopped in the doorway, appalled. Dirty dishes were piled in the sink. The floor was unswept. Blinds drawn. His brother, his face unshaven, was watching some video or movie on his iPad.

"What the hell happened? Why didn't Clarissa clean?"

"Oh, I told her not to bother. That I'd do it." Erik blinked around him, mole-like, seeming surprised at the mess. "I didn't want her to have to deal with it since there's kind of a lot."

"Uh, yeah, kind of." He stood watching his brother, hands on his hips. "Allie was supposed to be here by now."

"And?"

Jonas gestured to the mess. "And you want her to see this?"

"Uh…" Erik gave him a look as if he was speaking some other language. "I don't really think it matters one way or the other."

"Did you wash a single dish all week?"

"Hey." Erik closed his iPad. "My dishwashing pace is my business."

"In your own house. Not one we share."

"Lighten up, dude. No rape, no murder and no kidnapping happened here. I will wash the dishes. The kitchen will be clean."

"Are you still in your bathrobe?"

Erik chuckled, shaking his head. "Yes, *Dad*."

Jonas saw red for a moment. He would really like to punch his brother in the nose. "I wouldn't have to be like this if you'd taken ten minutes to—"

He locked his jaw shut, appalled that Erik was right. He sounded exactly like their dad.

For a tense few seconds he stared at his brother, still wanting to punch him, but recognizing that maybe Erik was a trigger, not the underlying problem.

"Okay." He let out the breath he'd been holding. "You're right. I'm sounding exactly like him. God, Erik, I'm losing my shit."

"Yeah? Welcome to the club. I can't find mine anywhere, either."

Jonas had his hands halfway up to his face when what his brother said hit him, and instead of holding his aching head, he burst out laughing, pleased as hell when Erik joined him. They hadn't laughed together in a long time.

"You want to go for a run?" He automatically prepared himself for Erik's refusal. "I need to get rid of this bad energy."

"Sure."

Jonas gaped at him. "Yeah?"

"What, you think I don't know how to run?"

"Hey, I wasn't sure." Jonas grinned. "I'll change and meet you outside."

Five minutes later, in his running shorts and shoes, Jonas was surprised to find Erik dressed and waiting. And even more surprised when he set a moderate pace and his brother was able to keep up. "You been running in the city?"

"Some. Mostly the gym."

Gym? Erik? "Since when?"

"Since I found out Allie runs."

Jonas snorted. "Everything for the women, huh?"

"Been meaning to ask, Jonas, how come you're here this weekend?"

"Yeah, yeah, okay. Touché." They turned north on tree-lined Lake Shore Drive, aka Route 9, which meandered along the western shore of the lake.

"I'd say the woman has you."

"Nobody *has* me. I'm just up here because—"

"You can't stop thinking about her, because you have this intense craving for her body and the way she smells and smiles and speaks and—"

"For God's sake, Erik. You sound like you're in a movie."

"But I'm right."

He was. But Jonas wasn't going to admit it. "I'm here because we need to talk seriously about selling the house."

"What is *wrong* with you?" Erik stopped, then threw up his hands and sprinted to catch up when Jonas kept running. "Why can't you admit you're falling for her?"

"I'm not you."

"I noticed." He cleared his throat, breathing heavily now. "I'm falling for Sandra."

"Yeah?" Jonas feigned surprise. "Cool. Who's it going to be next week?"

"I'm serious, man." His voice was so somber, Jonas glanced over at him. He did look serious. Or maybe the run was about to give him a heart attack. "I've never felt this way about any woman. I think this is it."

"Come on." Jonas slowed his pace to go easier on his brother. "Last week you said that about Allie."

"That was different. I wanted to marry Allie because I thought it was time I got married and that she'd be good for me. Comfortable, you know. Like old clothes." He looked over at Jonas apologetically. "No offense."

"None taken." Though Erik's thinking that someone as unpredictable and exciting as Allie was comfortable was like…well, like the way Jonas had thought about settling down with Sandra.

What had seemed pleasant and possible back then would now feel like settling, not settling down.

They ran on, passing the boat store where Dad had bought their kayaks, a few houses of neighbors he'd met and enjoyed. It would be hard to give this place up.

"I think I'm in love with her." Erik betrayed his agitation by speeding nearly to a sprint.

"Erik." Jonas couldn't believe what he'd just heard. Over the years his brother had used every word in the dictionary to describe his feelings for women. All except for that one. "Did you just say you think—"

"No, I don't think. I *am* in love with her." His voice was thick with emotion. "What the hell am I going to do?"

"Do? You're asking *me?*" Jonas started laughing. "I couldn't even admit why I came up here this weekend."

"What is wrong with us?" Erik was laughing, too. "I mean, really, this emotion stuff shouldn't be so hard. We grew up in *such* an open and supportive family."

"Oh, *yeah*." Between running and laughing, Jonas could barely get the words out. "Every night at dinner it was the same from Dad, 'Jonas, Erik, please share your feelings with your mother and me.'"

"Ha!" Erik could barely catch his breath. "Yes! 'We would like to listen with respect and then validate those emotions, so we will never ever make you feel as if you couldn't possibly measure up to our standards.'"

"'Afterward, your mother and I would like to share *our* feelings. We'll admit we're only human and let you off the hook for being that way, too.'"

"'What's that, Erik?'" Erik put a hand to his ear as if he were their father listening to a distant voice. "'You think I can be a narrow-minded, intolerant son of a bitch? *Thank you* for sharing that.'"

Jonas ran faster, feeling as if he were on the verge of bursting out of some too-tight shell. "'What, Jonas? Did you say you were effing tired of being responsible all the time? Go wild! Please let your mother and I know how we can help with your quest for self-knowledge and fulfillment.'"

Erik dropped behind while a car passed them. "Can you imagine?"

"Not really."

They ran on, past woods, mowed lawns, occasional houses or businesses, no longer chuckling.

"Though in the end, it's too easy to blame our parents." Jonas used his shirt to wipe his forehead. "They did their best. It's up to us to be who we want to be."

"True." Erik was starting to sound winded. "Me? I want to be a man in bed with Sandra for the rest of my life."

"So drive to Boston and tell her."

Erik stopped abruptly. Jonas turned back after momentum carried him a few more steps. Erik stood, panting, looking as if he'd just been zapped with electricity.

"What am I, a moron?"

Jonas winced. "Dude, don't hand me that one."

"Drive to Boston. Why did that never occur to me?"

"That initiative thing…"

"Yeah, not my strong point." Erik shook his head, leaning forward, hands braced on his thighs. "What's even scarier is that *you* are the one who had to tell me to be spontaneous."

"I planned it." Jonas waved dismissively. "It's in my date book. Five-seventeen p.m. Tell Erik to be spontaneous."

Erik straightened and gave Jonas a high five. "C'mon, let's go back."

"What, now?" Jonas gestured to the road ahead. "We barely did a mile! This highway ends in Canada."

"Ha! Race you to the house."

Jonas sprang into action, beating his brother, but not by as much as he'd expected. Erik had been taking this working-on-himself thing seriously. Jonas hadn't given him enough credit.

"Hey." He socked Erik on the shoulder, the closest he and his brother got to a hug. "You're really serious about getting your life under control. I'm proud of you."

Erik tried to hide his grin under eye-rolling, but it was clear

Jonas's comment pleased him. "And you—you're really losing control, dude. *I'm* proud of *you*."

It was Jonas's turn to roll his eyes. He wasn't quite sure his brother's comment had pleased him the same way, but he knew what Erik meant. "Yeah, we'll see."

"I'm going to shower and pack. Allie coming soon?"

"A couple of hours."

"Cool." He started for the house, then paused and turned back to give Jonas a brief hug. "I love you, man."

"Jeez, Erik." Jonas grinned, meeting his brother's eyes so he'd know the words had touched him, though he had too much of his dad in him to answer. "Meyer men don't— What am I supposed to say to that?"

"Just one thing." Erik held up his hand, backing toward the house, grinning. "That you'd be happy to clean up the kitchen."

CHAPTER TWELVE

STILL DRIPPING from an unexpected rain shower, Sandra let herself into her tiny apartment—a crappy place in a decent neighborhood in Somerville, but she insisted on living alone, and this was what she could afford.

Her show tonight had been grim. The bar was only half-full, half of the people there weren't listening to her songs and some drunk guy in a cowboy hat kept making obnoxious comments. *That song is as old as my grandma. Play* Freebird. *I wanna refund.* Nights like this she was ready to give up the whole career.

She dumped her bag on the kitchen table and kicked her flip-flops onto the orange-and-brown shag carpet, which must have looked clean and new at some point, but she couldn't imagine it had ever looked good.

A quick shower later, she wrapped herself up in a thin cotton robe and contemplated the contents of her refrigerator. A few eggs. A hunk of cheese with white mold on one corner.

Forget it. She wasn't hungry.

She missed Erik.

Sandra slammed the refrigerator door closed. Damn it, this was not supposed to have happened. They were supposed to have fun; she was supposed to teach him a lesson about respecting women, about being a real man like his brother instead of a live-for-the-moment boy. And in the process, he was supposed to get the idea of marrying her and turn her life of struggle into easy street, while she gave him the combination of stability he craved and wildness he needed.

Somehow he'd turned the tables on her, gotten her to open up, tell him things she'd told nobody, made her vulnerable to him in a way she hadn't been vulnerable since her mom and dad kicked her out of the house when she needed them most. What kind of parents let their seventeen-year-old daughter marry a thirty-year-old she'd known for six weeks? And then punish her by disowning her, as if she'd been old enough to make a wise decision on her own?

She'd sworn she'd never need anyone like that again. So far she'd done well. Her marriage had been an act of rebellion. Edwin hadn't been able to touch her, nor had Jake or any boyfriend since, with the possible exception of Jonas. But even he had never gotten to her like this.

When she left Erik yesterday morning—keeping their goodbye casual, thanking him for the wild time, and telling him she hoped she'd see him again soon—she'd been dying inside. Then and all the way home. That drunk cowboy tonight probably deserved a refund. Most likely what sucked about her show was her. She'd been going through the motions.

Damn it.

Erik hadn't said he'd call her, or text her, or given any indication that he'd like to see her again. And right there she was pissed. Why should she care? She had never been and never wanted to be the kind of woman who fretted over crap like that; she didn't need to fret over it this time. Two secrets had been told so far. After the third, he got sex. He'd call.

Or maybe she'd scared him away.

Tuesday night after Allie left, Jonas had been around, and they'd had an uproarious evening drinking and telling stories until late. Wednesday she and Erik had been alone, and after a delicious dinner with excellent wine, they'd continued their game. He'd told her he'd once slept with a married woman he was crazy about, and then she freaked out and went back to her husband, leaving him brokenhearted and totally disgusted with himself.

Then it was her turn. She'd started fine, telling him briefly about her impulsive marriage to a controlling man, and her escape from him into the world of exotic dancing. This time she would stay cool. She understood every level of what she'd done, and he couldn't turn this one back on her.

He hadn't. She'd broken down all by herself. Because instead of being shocked or titillated, Erik had been immediately sympathetic, imagining the betrayal she'd felt when her marriage became unbearable, the frustration of turning to dancing for a

living when she wanted to be taken seriously as a vocal artist…
Whether it was the wine or not, Sandra had come undone. She'd
told him everything. Her stories, all the truths, all her power had
poured out of her. How her dancing had been thrilling at first,
how she'd reveled in the power over men after feeling victim to
Edwin for nearly five years. Then the boredom, the dissatisfac-
tion, the drugs, the man who tempted her with the money she
could make as an "escort." How close she'd come to doing just
that, leaving the first guy without taking his money. Her subsequent struggle to get out and get clean.

Sandra had only cried a few times in her life. When her parents disinherited her. When she left her husband. When she woke
up after her first and only night as a call girl. And that night in
front of poor Erik who hadn't signed on for anything more than
a flirtatious game with a tough girl from Southie.

Yes, to correct her misstep, she'd initiated a fabulous full-body
make-out session that left Erik crazy with lust, back where she
wanted him. But Thursday morning she'd gotten a call to cover
for a singer she owed favors to, and she'd had to leave, without
being sure the damage control was complete.

Now here she was, missing the bastard, terrified he had her
under his power as much as he was under hers. Or the unthink-
able—maybe more.

Somewhere in her kitchen cabinet was a really nice bottle of
wine a drunk bar manager had given her a few months back,
which she'd saved for a special occasion. At the time she'd hoped
it would be a happy one. But maybe this was more appropriate.

She'd just extracted the cork and was about to pour when her
phone rang.

Yeah, whoever it was could just screw him-or herself.

Maybe it was Erik.

She rolled her eyes and poured. Yeah, or Gerard Butler.

The phone kept ringing.

It wasn't going to be Erik.

Except it might be.

She stared at the bottle, at the single glass of wine next to it…
and yanked the phone out of her pocket.

It was Erik.

"Sandra. How was the show?"

"Dismal." She was instantly fizzy inside, having become an utter fool. Hearing his voice was like being given a big drink when you were thirsty—with no idea when the next drink would be coming or how long the supply would last.

"Sorry to hear that. Hey, is that your doorbell? I'll wait while you answer."

She looked in confusion at the apartment's buzzer. "No."

"I heard it ring."

"Must have been something on your end."

"Nope. Yours. Or maybe it hasn't happened yet. I'm psychic, you know."

Sandra narrowed her eyes. "Have you been drinking?"

"Not yet."

Her buzzer rang. Sandra jumped about a mile. "Holy Mary, mother of God, the doorbell."

"Told you. Go answer it."

"Well, I… What the hell is going on?" She stepped over to the buzzer and pressed it cautiously. Had he orchestrated some kind of delivery? "Hello?"

"Hey. Let me up."

"Erik." Her jaw dropped. She laughed in disbelief. "Okay. You got me. How did you get here?"

"Drove like a demon."

"You can't come up, I'm not dressed."

"I'm sorry, were you expecting me to object to that?"

Sandra grinned, shaking her head, and pressed the button to let him into the building. Erik was here. He'd driven *four hours* to see her.

She rushed into the bathroom and put on the barest hints of eyeliner and blush. The apartment was a fourth-floor walk-up. It would take him a while to—

The knock came on her door. He must have run up.

She rushed to answer, then forced herself to slow down. *Whoa, wait a second, girl.* Sandra from Southie didn't go all flustered and silly for anyone, least of all a guy. She'd made that one mistake, letting down her guard. It appeared she wouldn't have to pay for that, but she'd be sure not to make another.

Centering herself, she arranged her features into utter calm and opened the door. "Well, well, Mr. Meyer."

He was gorgeous. Rain had dampened and darkened his hair, and the humidity had curled it slightly. His eyes stood out, blue and intense, in the dim hallway. He held a grocery bag in one hand and a bouquet of mixed roses in the other, as if he was an old-fashioned gentleman come courting.

She loved it.

"Hi there." He gave her a casual kiss and strolled into her apartment, looking around, not betraying any reaction. "I brought us a late supper."

"What are you doing here?" She closed the door behind him, thinking how wrong he looked here, how out of place anywhere but a mega-mansion.

"I missed you." He put the groceries on her table.

"Really." He *missed* her! This was good. A relief, really. She hadn't blown it. She'd just have to be careful today. And every day.

His eyes darted around again, from the groceries he was unloading to the orange shag. The scuffed cabinets. The linoleum counters with the metal strip bent and peeling off one corner. The garbage can she had to keep by the refrigerator because there was no room under the sink. The cracking paint. The tiny living room through a doorway on one end. The tinier bedroom on the other.

Sandra folded her arms across her chest. "Welcome to how the other half lives."

"Hey, it's a nice location." He folded the paper shopping bag and offered it to her.

"You can say it, you know." She took the bag and stuffed it in the crack between the refrigerator and sink where she kept the others.

"Say what?"

"That you're uncomfortable because you live in a palace and I live here."

He huffed. "You think that matters to me?"

Sandra pulled another wineglass from the cabinet, forming her answer carefully. "I would guess that you don't want it to matter, that intellectually it might not, but that coming here and looking around, you are fairly shocked and possibly repulsed."

He looked startled for a moment, then stepped to the table, poured a second glass of wine and held out the first for her, his eyes warm. "I'd say that once again you have cut through bullshit and forced me to acknowledge a subconscious truth. My mom constantly warned Jonas and me about women after our money. She never told us about women who'd hate it."

Sandra shrugged uneasily and gulped some wine, which she should be savoring sip by sip. Maybe it was just as well that he got the impression she hated his money. Though it made everything even more complicated. "So, what have you brought?"

"Ah." He reached toward the table and held up a baguette from the local organic food store, which she couldn't even afford to step into. "Basics. Bread, cheese, salads, plums and chocolate."

Locally made bread, foreign cheeses costing upward of twenty dollars a pound, deli salads with fresh artichokes and imported caper berries, organic plums and exclusive Hawaiian chocolate.

Her hunger had been renewed. For this meal, for that life… and for Erik.

They settled on her stained couch in the living room, food spread out on the coffee table she'd found at a rummage sale.

While they stuffed themselves, they chatted about her show, about Allie and Jonas, about Lake George, about Boston versus New York, until the bottle was empty, the food decimated.

"So, Sandra." Erik moved closer to her on the couch. "We have some unfinished business."

She sent him a withering look. "Did you *really* just use that line on me?"

"No." He shook his head violently. "Absolutely not. That was someone else."

Sandra giggled, buoyed by the wine and Erik's really fun company. "I believe you owe me one more secret."

"Do I?" He took her wine, put it down next to his, drew her to him and kissed her, gentle and sweet. He smelled amazing, of spice and leather. Her body responded—but so did her heart.

"I thought maybe we could do a short recap first of previous sexual—"

"Not so fast." Sandra told her heart to cut it out. "You owe me that secret first."

"And I intend to pay up." He put his hand to his heart, then took hers and pressed it there, as well. "But you have to go first this time."

Sandra snorted. "Why, you want to make me cry again?"

"Ah, but you cry like an angel."

"Ha!" She smiled unwillingly. "You've never seen one."

"Not until I met you."

Sandra ignored the piercing sweetness in her chest. "Save the lines for your other women."

"Ooh." He grimaced. "Unfortunately…there aren't any."

"No?" She pretended to be surprised, wanting desperately to smooth back hair that had fallen over his forehead.

He looked down at his hands clasping his wineglass. "I'm not sure what's happening to me, Sandra, but I'm starting to suspect you might be it for a while."

"Because…" Her heart started thumping. This was dangerous ground. "You're becoming a monk?"

"Never!"

"Oh." She patted his knee sympathetically. "Impotence, I understand."

He shot her a glance. "Just try me."

Sandra laughed, feeling twenty times better than she had an hour before, and swung her legs over his, easing into his lap. What had she been worrying about? Everything was back to the way it was. Everything was fine. "I don't think that's a good idea just yet."

He held her gaze, looking more serious than she'd ever seen him. Forget thumping, her heart was hammering now; instinct was warning her, fight or flight. "I want to make love to you, Sandra."

Lord have mercy.

She managed to keep her reaction mostly under control. Only

the smallest gasp leaked out. "Sorry, that wasn't the deal until after the third secret."

"I'm changing the rules." He pushed her legs off him, stood and dragged her to her feet with more force than he needed so she overbalanced. As she cried out, he bent down, catching her across his shoulders in a fireman's carry, and strode with her back into the kitchen.

"Oh for—" She was half laughing, half turned on by the macho act. "Put me down."

"Soon."

"I mean it, Erik."

"I know you do." A few more strides and they were in her bedroom. He knelt by her bed so she could dismount. Just as she straightened, ready to let him have it, he lunged up and tumbled her onto the mattress, covering her body with his.

"Well, Sandra." He grinned lazily down at her. "Here we are."

Her alarm bells were still sounding. His words echoed in her ears, *I want to make love to you, Sandra.* "Off me, you pig."

"Umm…no, thank you." He pushed her robe open and took in a sharp breath, gazing at her nakedness. "I have dreamed of you, Sandra, missed you, wanted you."

His words blasted through her attitude, and without that she could say nothing, just lay staring at the ceiling as his mouth found her breast. Then she closed her eyes, trying to lose herself in the sensation, telling herself he was flawed, mortal, not worthy of her goddess status, trying to remind herself that she was the great invincible Sandra, who'd never fall for any man, no matter how charmingly he presented himself. To give in to the warm, sweet feelings welling up in her would spell her doom, and the end of his interest.

No weakness.

He kissed down her stomach. Sandra waited, fists clenching the bedspread. The first lick was a long, slow caress. Then nothing. She stayed motionless, her arousal peaking, then dissipating. His tongue made the long, slow trip again. Again, she lay still, controlling her breathing and her heart as best she could.

Then touches, light ones, gentle flicks across her clit. Her breath caught. She suppressed a moan, forced herself not to move. Her desire shot up and hung like a firework in the sky, waiting to explode.

Then nothing but the room's cool air.

A whimper escaped her. Erik whispered her name, then slid a finger inside her, started the gentle touches and licks again, taking his time, bringing her nearly to the edge, backing off and letting her come down. She fought him, not wanting him to make her lose control, even this way.

"Come for me, Sandra." He was breathing fast, and his voice was low with emotion.

She shook her head. "You owe me a secret."

He got off the bed and began taking off his clothes. His emerging body was familiar, beautiful, not perfect, but muscled and totally masculine. She swallowed. Never in her wildest dreams did she think this game would turn out to be so deadly serious, the rules she'd made up as a way to manipulate him so threatening to her own peace of mind.

Then he was naked, except for a condom, getting back onto her double bed, pulling off her robe, laying her back down. She submitted, anxious, eager, reluctant, impatient, terrified.

She'd never made love to anyone she cared about this much. The realization brought tears to her eyes.

No, she couldn't do this.

"Erik…" She couldn't believe the fear in her voice. Where was Sandra the Southie now?

"Shhh." He kissed her, his erection warm and promising between her legs. "What is it? What are you afraid of?"

You. Me. What I feel for you. She shook her head. "The big bad wolf."

He chuckled. "You are bigger and badder than he can ever be."

"But I'm not…" She couldn't go on. Couldn't explain. He had no idea who she was or how she felt.

He stroked her hair back from her face, kissed her tenderly, laid his head down next to hers. "I'm going to tell you my secret. You said it had to be something I'd never told any other woman."

An instant before he spoke, she guessed what he was going to say, and her heart rose in panic. This was what her instinct was warning her about. This was the difference today. She'd spent her life building barriers against this moment, barriers that she had no idea how to take down, or if she even wanted to.

She struggled to get away from him, lifting her hips, trying to slide to one side, out from under his body. The movement gave him his chance—or maybe he misunderstood. He plunged inside her, making her cry out in pleasure and despair.

"Sandra." He pushed farther, gaining depth with each thrust until she felt he would take her over forever. "Sandra. God help me. I love you."

CHAPTER THIRTEEN

JONAS SWITCHED OFF the engine. Allie sent him a nervous smile and got out of the car immediately. The ride from the bus station had been torture. Julie had been wrong—it was a mistake to come here again this weekend. She should have waited until next week, when Jonas was back in Boston and she could pack up the clothes at her leisure with Erik's help, and bring them back to New York.

Seeing Jonas again was a mistake. When she'd gotten off the bus and seen him standing, waiting for her, tall and solid, even more handsome than she remembered, her heart had started pounding with equal amounts of joy and nerves, her smile had stretched to enormous proportions across her face—and so had his. They'd met with a bump of bodies, with arms flung around each other. Anyone watching would think it a passionate reunion of longtime lovers.

On the way to his car, he'd asked about her trip. She'd recounted her frustration with the delay. He'd talked about the traffic on the Massachusetts Turnpike. He'd loaded her bag, which he'd insisted on carrying, gentleman that he was, into the backseat while she asked about Erik and Sandra. They'd gotten into the car to drive the half-hour-plus to the house, he'd asked a few questions about her second interview, she'd asked him about his work...then conversation had all but lapsed.

Shouldn't they be chatting up a storm? Shouldn't there be hopes and dreams to share, special moments they wanted each other to know about? Should she tell him one of her brothers was arrested that afternoon for cocaine possession? That her mother had been on the phone to Allie for an hour, drunk and crying over her worthless children, and why wasn't Allie with her in her time of need, and why didn't she ever visit, was she ashamed of them? Allie had always thought she was too good for them, didn't she... and on and on and on until Allie had cut her off, saying she had to go. Then things got really ugly.

Yeah, that would get the weekend off to a rousing start.

The only way Allie had been able to cope was to shut it all out, pretend these were distant acquaintances, and she was a horrified stranger, hearing of their sad, sad circumstances.

Now what? She'd put on some antique outfit and pretend she was really into seducing a man she shouldn't be here to see?

"You must be starving." He lifted her overnight bag out of the car.

"Yes, I am." She would be if it weren't for the nerves clogging her stomach.

"I got us dinner." He pulled a plastic shopping bag from the car. "Some excellent sandwiches from a place not far from the station."

"Thank you. That was sweet."

He shut the car door, looking at her curiously. "You're welcome."

She came around to join him on the walk to the cottage, remembering their times there before, desperately wanting to get closer to him and to keep him farther away, feeling stuck in some emotional bog she hadn't asked for and didn't quite understand.

"You all right?" He led the way around to the lake side of the cottage. For the first time she thought she'd rather be in the larger house.

"Just tired." She cringed at the clichéd excuse. But what could she say? *I'm not sure why I'm here or what I expect to find or what you want from me or what I want from you or...* "I'm sure I'll feel better after I eat something."

"Coming up." He gestured at the deck where he'd laid out a table with silver candlesticks, beautiful blue-and-white china and crystal wineglasses. A low vase held an assortment of colorful zinnias.

For sandwiches.

She closed her eyes briefly. What was wrong with her? The table wasn't for sandwiches, it was for her, and she should be incredibly pleased that Jonas had gone to all the trouble to make their meal special.

"How beautiful."

"Thanks." He touched her shoulder. "Food's not special, but I wanted your welcome to be."

"It's…beautiful." She said that already. For heaven's sake.

"I'll get the wine."

While he was in the kitchen, Allie plunked herself in one of the chairs, staring out at the lake, feeling worse than ever. The nicest guy in the world was waiting on her hand and foot and she was being a petulant child. She owed him an apology, and a lot more effort to be good company.

Minutes later, he emerged again, holding a bottle of white wine, which he started pouring into their glasses. "Want to start with wine or just dig in?"

"Jonas…"

He looked up at the sound of her voice. For a second before he forced his features blank, she saw fear, and felt worse than ever.

"I'm sorry I'm behaving so badly. I think I must be worried about this job…"

He shrugged, clearly not satisfied with her answer, and handed her a glass. "I get it. It's exhausting facing a big life change."

"Yes." She took the glass and drank a polite sip. "Though it's not really that big. I mean it's the same job I was just doing. So it shouldn't…"

Jonas frowned. "Let's eat, okay?"

"Sure." She sat, wishing they weren't going to have to have this dinner, wishing she was in his arms, or back home without him, anywhere but this odd limbo.

The sandwiches he'd picked out were delicious: tuna with capers, onion and avocado; grilled eggplant with pesto and mozzarella; and roast beef with caramelized onions and arugula. As she feasted happily away, Allie began to cheer up.

"So whenever you're ready…" His blue gaze was steady on her, one dark curl blown nearly vertical in the breeze.

Her heart sped. "Yes?"

"You can tell me what's really wrong."

"Oh." Allie put down her sandwich, lowered her eyes. "I guess the job thing wasn't that convincing."

"Nope." The syllable was clipped.

"I'm sorry." She pushed back from the table, unable to stand its confinement, taking her half-finished wine with her, and stood at the railing, thinking of the last two times she stood there, in fabulous silk and in sexy sequins. How different from tonight.

Jonas came to stand next to her. He put an arm around her, then let it drop. The message was clear. He wasn't touching her until he knew what was on her mind. She didn't blame him. "The thing is…"

"Go on."

She made a noise of exasperation and turned to face him. "I don't even *know* what the thing is."

"Try me. Whatever comes to mind."

"Okay." She drank more wine, aware that was probably a poor idea. "First, I don't know what's going on here with you and me, whether it's a good idea or not, whether it will work or not, what it even *is*."

"But…" He touched her shoulder, a slight caress. "We don't know each other well enough to pin any of that down yet."

"Right. Right." Okay, there went that excuse. "So then I don't know what will happen going forward. Do we date? Long distance? Which city? And how do we—"

"Allie."

"What?" Her frustration came out in the word.

He chuckled, looking gorgeous, his eyes full of amusement at her expense, as he took her wine away and balanced it on the railing.

"What is so funny?"

In answer he drew her close and kissed her the way he hadn't yet this time, not at the bus station with a crowd around them, not when they arrived and she was being so skittish, but the way he had when he'd gathered her in his arms right here at this railing after he'd made love to Cleopatra, and she thought it was the last time.

Her irritation melted. Her heart slowed, her muscles relaxed. She shut down her brain and responded to him with her body.

That was better. Much better. This could be okay. If they stayed in bed all weekend long doing what they did best, and she could keep from thinking and feeling too much, that was all she needed.

"Jonas." She tipped her head to allow him better access to her neck. "I need to go up to the attic."

"Why?" He found the perfect spot, where her shoulder ended and neck began, and brushed his lips across her skin.

"Page thirty-five," she whispered. "You wouldn't believe what Josephine—"

"Allie." He lifted his head, took her by the shoulders. "I don't want to make love to my great-grandmother. I want to make love to you."

She blinked, laughed uneasily. "Well yes, but—"

"No costume. Just you and me upstairs together. In my bed."

Allie's heart started again its slow, steady thump of anxiety. "Just us."

"Uh." He looked justifiably disbelieving. "Yeah?"

"I'm sorry." She pressed her hands to her temples. "I sound like an idiot."

"Uh-huh."

"Well maybe not an idiot. A ditz anyway."

"You said it."

She frowned at him. "Seriously, Jonas, you can contradict me anytime."

"Nope." He found her hand and drew her toward the cottage door. "Don't need to. You're doing fine."

"It's just that I'd envisioned the whole thing." She resisted his pull, but only slightly. "The nightgown you saw me in…"

"No nightgown." He led her across to the staircase.

"And then underneath, all she has on is this frilly little—"

"No frilly." He started climbing the stairs. "No little."

Allie started giggling. "But the shoes!"

"No shoes." In the bedroom he practically dragged her across the room.

"Jonas! You'd like the hat!"

"No." He swung her up in his arms and dumped her onto the mattress. "Hat."

She barely got control of her laughter. "Okay, okay."

"Clothes." He pointed to hers. "Off."

"Yes, sir." Allie sat up, watching him pull off his shirt, watching that magnificent chest emerge. She pulled off her top, one of her favorites, short-cropped with wildly colorful vertical stripes.

"Those, too." He pointed to her white capris, unbuttoned his jeans and shoved them down, rescuing a condom from the back pocket.

Allie scooted out of her pants, kicked her flip-flops off the bed and lay back in her bra and panties, arms folded across her chest, looking at him expectantly.

Except she couldn't keep her eyes from wandering down from his face. Broad muscular shoulders, defined abs, lean hips, powerful thighs and a half-erect penis that was calling to her.

Mmmm.

"Take off the rest, Allie." His hands were on his hips. He was looking...hungry. "Slowly."

She hesitated, strangely reluctant now that their laughter was over. "Can you get on the bed with me?"

He shook his head. "I want to watch you undress."

It hit her with a sudden shock that he'd never seen her naked. And that his request was perfectly natural. And that what she'd done in the costumes would lead him to believe she was totally comfortable in her body.

Well, wasn't she? She didn't exactly need the lights out when making love. So what was her problem now?

She smiled at Jonas, shook back her hair and sat halfway up to unhook her bra, sliding the straps slowly off each shoulder, letting her breasts emerge gradually into the cool air.

He inhaled. His erection grew. Clearly he liked what he saw. So why this intense shyness on her part?

She lay back on her elbows and passed her hands over her panties, pausing to rest her hands on the material between her legs, hoping he'd find that erotic, delaying the moment, feeling an unaccountably deep sense of anxiety and foreboding she didn't understand.

"Off." His lips were twisted in a small smile. He thought she was teasing him.

"If you insist." Her voice came out thick and strange. She edged the material down, bent her knees with pointed toes, and let the cotton slip down and off.

She'd been without clothes around men before, but had never, ever felt so naked.

"You're beautiful, Allie." He stood watching as if he had no intention of ever moving.

This wasn't part of their game. This wasn't a game at all.

"Come here." She held out her arms, hoping that as soon as he was there with her, as soon as he started kissing and touching her, her unease would disappear.

He climbed onto the bed with her and drew her close. She burrowed into the warm, soft feel of his skin, into the wide expanse of his back under her fingers, and the delicious weight of him pressing against her. The fear was still there, though it had diminished some. Why hadn't she felt this before? When she was Cleopatra? When she was the cool-as-cucumber seductress?

Because now she was just Allie.

He pressed her gently onto her back and explored her. Slowly, thoroughly with lips, fingers and tongue. Her face, her shoulders, then her belly and legs, then up again to dote on her breasts. Allie lay as she'd been instructed to, trying to relax. He was a skilled and patient lover. She was a rock.

When he concentrated his attention between her legs, Allie closed her eyes and imagined the nightgown still covered her, imagined she was a woman of elegance, with many, many lovers, of which Jonas was her favorite. Imagined he'd pushed up the wispy cotton batiste to kiss her as he was doing now.

Her arousal rose under the strokes of his tongue until she was again at the panting level of lust she'd experienced only with him.

"I want to make love to you," her dashing lover said.

"Yes." She waved her hand to give him permission.

Jonas entered her slowly, lazily, a bit at a time, in and out while she made room for him inside her, getting hotter and wetter until she was able to take him all.

Then he lay still, joined to her in the most intimate way of all, and waited until she opened her eyes to find him looking deeply into them.

Immediately she froze, staring back up at him as if his gaze were paralyzing her. Slowly, she began to recognize the man in the depths of those eyes, and felt herself responding. The connection became nearly unbearable, the emotions overwhelming. She felt torn apart, wanting to disappear into him, wanting to shut him out.

And then he began to move, faster and faster, with his eyes locked on hers. She bucked up against his thrusts, whimpering at the torture and pleasure of this invasion of her body and of her heart.

Then her orgasm was simply inevitable; her body began gathering for it, climbing steadily toward ecstasy. She closed her eyes, hissing breath through her teeth, moaning softly.

"Look at me when you're coming, Allie."

She couldn't, shook her head. It was too much, giving him too much. "I can't."

"Look at me." He spoke sharply, grinding his pelvis on hers, then moved out and plunged in again, nearly sending her over the edge. *"Look at me."*

She met his eyes, losing total control as he thrust again and her orgasm hit, making her shout, clutching his shoulders, writhing underneath him, feeling as if she couldn't get close enough to him even as close as they were.

Jonas!

"Allie." He whispered her name as if he'd heard her internally screaming his. She felt him strain, stiffen, then pulse inside her, his eyes locked onto hers again, insisting she share the pleasure she'd given him. Then they lay face-to-face, mouths open, panting, and if the look in Jonas's face was anything like hers, awed.

He dropped his head next to hers, pressing their cheeks together, digging his hands under her back to hold her tightly against him. She squeezed her eyes shut and tried to memorize the feeling of his body on hers. She was still experiencing aftershocks from her orgasm that triggered more in him, their bodies coming down together. Slowly her breathing returned to normal. She felt the oddest combination of ripped open and triumphant.

Was anything simple where Jonas was concerned?

"Mmm." He lifted his head. "Am I crushing you?"

She shook her head, smiling up at him.

"That was amazing, Allie. I'm—" He closed his eyes, shook his head briefly. "It was really wonderful."

"Yes." She was shy again, but not nearly as shy as before.

Jonas pulled reluctantly out of her, used tissues to dispose of the condom, and rolled back, pulling her against his chest. "Still want to get dressed up?"

"Hmm." She tangled her leg in his, knowing it was what he wanted to hear, then immediately prodding herself to tell him the truth. "Maybe sometimes."

"It was hard to talk you out of this time."

Allie shrugged, stroking the hair upward on his chest. This would be harder. "I guess I felt that without the clothes, it was just me."

He was silent for so long that she lifted her head to see his face. He was looking at her incredulously. "You didn't think I wanted just you?"

"No." She frowned. "No, I didn't mean that."

"What did you mean?"

Allie moved restlessly, splaying her fingers against his sternum. "I meant…"

He tightened his hold on her. "Tell me. No bull. Just tell me."

She nodded, remembering the deep feeling of connection while they were making love, the openness in his eyes. And Julie, saying Allie was using her past as an excuse to keep men at a distance. And the costumes. Maybe the awkwardness between them had been her fault, for not sharing enough of who she was from the beginning.

In as few words as possible, she told him. About her family. Their house. Her father leaving for another woman and their new life of poverty. Her mother's descent into alcoholism. Her brothers' lack of ambition, and recent criminal activity.

He listened quietly. When she had the courage to glance up

at him, his expression was unreadable. Twice, she wanted to cut the story short, but forced herself to keep going, not to leave out anything crucial to who she really was.

When she finished, the silence was long and nearly unbearable.

Then he cleared his throat. "Why the shame, Allie?"

"Well it's—" She laughed bitterly. "It's not a pretty story."

"No, it's not. Why couldn't you tell me this from the beginning? When I asked questions about your childhood? You shut me out."

"I don't—" She took a breath. "It's not the kind of thing you can tell just anyone."

"Uh…"

"No. Jeez. No, that came out wrong." She gazed at him pleadingly. "You're not just anyone, of course you're not. But I hate that part of my life, I left it behind me for the most part. It's not just you, I hardly tell anyone. And frankly, the last guy I told dropped me immediately."

His eyes narrowed. "You think I'm the kind of person who would drop you because of something that happened twenty years ago? Because you don't have money? You think I'm that shallow?"

His words hit her like a kick to the stomach. Of course he'd see it that way. Who wouldn't? Why hadn't she realized how it would seem to him?

"No," she whispered. "I don't think you're that shallow. But I'm beginning to wonder if I am."

CHAPTER FOURTEEN

IT WAS A RELIEF to be back at work, with everything going as expected, everything under control. Jonas's weekend with Allie at Lake George had been anything but. Friday night, when he'd finally made love to her the way he'd wanted to from the moment he first met her in New York last Christmas, he'd been sure he was falling in love with her. He was even plotting to talk her out of taking the job in New York, and wondering how he could convince her to move to Boston. He'd like nothing better than to help support her while she started her own business, though he was well aware it was too soon to make those kinds of plans. He'd even fleetingly thought of starting his own company in New York, though it made little business sense given the wide array of contacts and clients he had here in Beantown. Still, in today's mobile world anything was possible.

When she'd told him about her situation growing up, almost everything had changed. He still found her incredibly desirable, he still loved being with her, laughing with her, making love to her.

But…

Her revelation underscored how little they knew each other. How much she'd been holding back. How little she trusted him or his reaction. How little she understood what his life was about, and how little he understood hers.

It was time to put on the brakes. Time to stop thinking he'd found true love and start thinking with his rational brain. The fact that he'd been considering changing his life for her or asking her to change her life for him after such a short time together had been crazy, irrational, something his brother would do.

And so damn thrilling. He'd felt alive, without having realized he'd been half dead; he felt the life ahead of him was newly full of possibilities, that with Allie beside him, he could conquer mountains, move armies. Or was that the other way around?

God, he missed her.

He picked up a report and scanned the first page, felt his irritation rising. Same old ineffective solutions to the same old problems. Cut management. Freeze wages. Come into work. Leave work. Go home alone.

Jonas closed the report and tossed it onto his desk, shoved back his chair, and strode to the window, yanking his tie loose. Head close to the glass, he peered up at the sliver of gray sky the view afforded him.

He couldn't stay here. Not when he had tasted the joy and freedom Allie brought him, even for such a short time.

The rest of the weekend with her had been dismal. Neither of them had recovered from her revelation. He was hurt, she felt rejected, and though they'd tried to rehash the subject a few times, their conversations were too accusing, too emotional, the gap too wide. No matter how many times he reassured her that he couldn't care less where she came from, that her real self was what mattered to him, she didn't buy it. Because he had money she assumed he looked down on her, that he was unable to judge her as a whole person.

And no matter how much he tried, he couldn't get over the way she'd judged him, or the way he'd fallen for someone who wasn't what he thought. Again.

Ironically, they both wanted the same thing: someone who would love them for who they were.

His phone rang. Sandra. Perfect example. Sandra was from humble beginnings, but at least she'd been honest, and was proud of being that person. He didn't know many people who were more comfortable in their own skin, more sure of who they were.

He picked up the phone eagerly. "Hey, there."

"You hungry, baby?"

"Only for you."

Her laughter sounded forced. "Can you meet for lunch? I can be at your building in ten minutes."

Jonas looked at his watch. "It's not even eleven."

"Oh, right, I forgot, we're not allowed to eat until noon because that's when lunchtime starts."

He rolled his eyes at her sarcasm. She knew him too well.

"Okay, okay, I'll meet you in ten minutes. Sandwich place across the street?"

"See ya there."

She was waiting when he walked into the small, cheerful café, looking tired but beautiful as ever in a hot-pink top with her hair loosely pinned up. He kissed her cheek and sat opposite, wondering what was on her mind, guessing it had something to do with his brother. If Erik had hurt her…

"How was your weekend?"

"Oh, fine, fine. Let's see." She tapped her cheek, looking thoughtful. "Friday I had a quiet afternoon, did a show, came home, took a shower, poured wine…oh, and then your brother came over and told me he loved me."

Jonas grinned. "Yeah?"

She stared at him, her lips parted in surprise. "You knew."

"He told me."

"He *told* you?"

Jonas reached for his water and shrugged nonchalantly. "Hey, I'm his brother. He tells me everything."

Sandra snorted. "Since when?"

"Since he told me he's in love with you and I told him to get his ass to Boston and tell you." He reached across the table to squeeze her hand. "He means it, Sandra."

"He certainly thinks he—"

"*Hey,* there!" A young waitress came beaming over to their table. "How are you two doing on this sunny Monday?"

"We're fine." Sandra shot Jonas a look. She loathed hyper-cheerful waitresses.

"Oka-a-y! My name is Amanda, and I'll be taking care of you today!"

"I can take care of myself, Amanda." Sandra accepted her menu wearily. "From you, I just need lunch."

"Oh. Well, okay, sure, no problem, I can do that." She giggled nervously, took their orders for iced tea and fled.

Jonas nodded pointedly toward Amanda's retreat. "Nice."

"I'm not feeling very nice today."

"You *look* very nice."

She smiled. "You're adorable. I wish I could marry you and be done with all this."

"Huh?" His brother must have rattled her badly. The Sandra he knew would have either patted Erik's head and sweetly told him to go away, or she would have laughed until he left on his own. "What did you do when he told you he loved you?"

"What any closeted romantic would do. I freaked the hell out."

"In a good way or bad?"

Sandra dropped her eyes. "Both."

Really. How interesting. "How did Erik react?"

"Like any Meyer out for what he wants. He shrugged and said I might as well get used to it because he wasn't going anywhere." Her features softened. "I'm feeling doomed."

"There are worse fates." He grimaced playfully. "Though given Erik, I'm not sure I want to know what they are."

"Ha!" She sipped her iced tea, blushing.

Blushing! Sandra! Jonas grinned, suddenly able to imagine Sandra as a future sister-in-law.

"So…" She looked at him expectantly. "Allie. What's going on there?"

"Nothing at the moment."

"Wait, why?" Her anguish was genuine. "I thought you guys were perfect for each other."

"I thought so, too. Until Friday."

"Oh, God." Sandra lifted her iced tea. "Hell of a day for lovers. What happened?"

"She told me things about her past." He shook his head. "It's hard to explain."

Across from him Sandra stiffened. "What kind of things?"

"She grew up poor. Really bad. Her dad left the family for a rich woman, her mom slid into alcoholism, her five brothers ran wild, it was really…tough."

"Sounds it. So what was the problem?"

"She never told me. It was like she didn't trust I could handle it. What kind of person does that make me?"

Sandra looked at him through narrowed eyes for so long that he started to wonder if she'd been listening. "Got a cigarette?"

"Huh?" Her request startled him. "I don't smoke. And neither do you."

"Used to. Gave it up when I gave up amphetamines and stripping, which I started after I left my abusive husband whom I married to escape my billionaire parents, the McKinleys of Greens Farms, Connecticut."

He waited for her to laugh, to let him in on the joke, and when she didn't, he could only stare. Had she lost it? "Sandra…"

"It was a while ago." She picked up the menu, clearly having a hard time. "What looks good to you here?"

"Wait, are you serious? About all…that?"

She met his eyes. "Deadly."

He sat back in his chair, bewildered. Two bombshells in three days from the women he was closest to. What the hell? "You never told me."

"Nope."

"Why not?"

"It's not the kind of thing you just tell someone."

Jonas winced. Her words were nearly identical to the ones Allie had used. "It *is* the kind of thing you tell a close friend."

"I just did."

"But—"

"Jonas, it was a long time ago, it sucked, now it's over."

"Yeah, but…" He narrowed his eyes, trying to put all these crazy pieces together into something that made sense. "Have you told Erik?"

"Friday."

"Why him? Why Friday and not before?"

"I think I'll have the BLT burger." She stabbed her finger at a spot on the page. "I need to ingest fat and protein in large quantities."

"You told him…" Jonas felt like the wheels were only just starting to turn in his brain. "Because he was a lot more than a good friend."

"Let's not jump to conclusions."

"Holy moly, Sandra." He stared at her, alternating between disbelief and happiness for both of them. "I'm speechless."

"Actually, you're still talking." She closed her menu and set it down carelessly, but he saw her trying to hold back a smile.

"Hey, there! How are those iced teas working for you?"

"How are they *working* for us?" Sandra feigned confusion. "Oh, wait, you mean how do they taste?"

"They're fine, Amanda, thanks." Jonas shot Sandra a cut-it-out look, wanting Amanda gone so he could take his conversation with Sandra to the next logical, amazing, wonderful step.

"Good! Good!" Amanda's smile had finally lost some of its wattage. Jonas would give her a huge tip. "May I take your orders?"

"I'll have the BLT cheeseburger, medium, with the seasoned fries and coleslaw." Sandra handed the menu back and blinked sweetly at Jonas—*See? I wasn't mean that time.*

"I'll have…" Jonas picked up the menu and glanced at it. "The same."

"Gre-e-at! I'll have those right out for you."

Jonas waited impatiently for Amanda to walk away, and then leaned across the table, his head whirling, heart pounding. "I didn't go far enough before. You actually told Erik the truth about yourself on Friday because you're in *love* with him."

She waggled her index finger back and forth. "Not admitting that."

"C'mon, Sandra."

"I told him because he has this superpower that makes me tell him things I'm not intending to." Her voice thickened. "And then after I do, I feel closer to him, and then vulnerable and terrified and I swear I'll never do it again. And then I do. I think I'm cracking up."

"That would explain—" Jonas clapped his hand to his head. "God, I'm an idiot."

Sandra snorted. "If the trouble between you and Allie is your fault, no argument there."

"No big trouble. Just a snag." He drew his hands down his face, suddenly filled with all the energy he'd been missing over the weekend. "So how did you and Erik leave it?"

"We just left it." She sighed. "Still stuff to deal with. How did you and Allie leave it?"

"We just left it." He sighed. "Still stuff to deal with. But you know, if things don't work out with Erik, you'll always have me."

She patted his hand. "If you don't make things work with Allie you're a moron who doesn't deserve any happiness for the rest of time."

Jonas smiled tenderly. "Aw, thanks, babe."

"Here we go!" Amanda put down their burgers. "Will there be anything else?"

Sandra picked up her burger. "There might be someday."

"Nothing, thank you," Jonas said. "Ignore her, she's on leave from the clinic."

"Ah!" Amanda threw her head back and laughed extremely loudly, then walked quickly away.

Sandra smiled affectionately at Jonas, a real sweet smile, brimming with affection. He smiled back.

"I want you to be happy, Jonas."

"I want you to be happy, too."

"Good. Enough sentiment." She gestured to their burgers. "Time to harden our arteries."

"Absolutely." He picked up his burger and took a fabulous juicy bite. "And then I need to make some serious plans."

Diary, my dreams all came true tonight—not the way I planned, but does it really matter? After Walter came in from nighttime fishing on the lake with his friend Ted, I was going to meet him at the door of his room wearing the absolutely fabulous white beaded lace dress that I got for my birthday but haven't worn yet, and underneath it, white lace knickers. To give him a taste of the sweet virginal girl I can be.

But it didn't work out that way. Ted got sick, so Walter invited me out instead, for a romantic ride. Of course I couldn't wear the dress in a rowboat! But he didn't seem to mind. He rowed me out to the middle of the lake, and then he brought out candles and a bottle of dessert wine and some wonderful cakes he'd bought in Glens Falls. It was so beautiful and so romantic.

When we'd had enough to eat, and probably too much to drink, Walter got on his knees and proposed! I nearly fell overboard. I am so very, very happy, and so much in love. We want our children to come up here with us every summer and grow to love the place as much as we do.

Walking on air tonight!

ALLIE CLOSED AND LATCHED the last trunk in the attic. Jonas and Erik had arranged for a moving company to stop by midweek to pick up the clothes and deliver them to Julie's parents' apartment in New York, which had enough storage space. The idea of starting her own shop appealed to her—either online or in an actual, physical space—using the clothes from the attic as inspiration for her own creations. In the meantime, she'd accepted the new job that morning and would start the following Monday. Since there wouldn't be much of a learning curve, her hope was that she'd have time to work on her new career, though crunch times during any ad campaign meant long hours in the office. Just the idea made her feel claustrophobic. But the reality of her situation was that she needed a job. The people seemed nice there, and they'd been pleased she accepted the offer. It was the right thing to do.

She stood and indulged in a good stretch, freezing at a noise downstairs. Was someone here? The mysterious Clarissa? Or Erik, back from Boston? He wasn't due back until tomorrow. She hoped he and Sandra had a good time, and that he'd be bringing her with him for his second week of vacation. Funny to think how so recently he'd wanted to spend those two weeks alone with her.

Footsteps sounded below.

"Hello?" she called over toward the trapdoor, her silly, over-optimistic heart hoping it was Jonas, while at the same time she scolded herself for being ridiculous. After that strained horrible weekend together she'd be surprised if he ever wanted to see her again.

Julie had sure been right! Unlocking the truth about Allie's past had set a whole lot of stuff in motion that was making her really, really happy! Which was why she'd cried herself to sleep the previous night.

Come to think of it, she hoped it wasn't Jonas. She looked like a puffy-eyed clown.

"Hey, girlfriend."

"Sandra!" She was desperately happy to hear Sandra's voice, feeling suddenly as if she was stuck in a snowbank and Sandra had a keg of rum around her neck.

"What's going on?" Sandra's beautiful face and shoulders appeared through the hole in the floor, followed by the rest of her. Even in jeans and a simple blue striped top, she looked exotic and glamorous. Immediately Allie could tell something was different about her, but couldn't figure out what. "Oh, you're packing up! What did you decide to do?"

"Nothing for a while." She shrugged dismissively. "I had thoughts about starting my own business designing clothes."

"You should! If your designs look anything like these clothes you'll be huge."

"Thanks." Allie smiled, wondering how Sandra could have that much confidence in her when she'd never seen anything Allie had designed. More confidence than Allie had in herself. She gestured impulsively to one of Bridget's trunks. "Listen, I was going to offer anyway, but didn't know you'd be here before I left. Would you like some of the gowns for your shows?"

"Oh, you are a sweetheart. Thank you." Sandra's eyes brightened. "Tell you what, you start your shop and I'll be your first and best customer."

Allie nodded her thanks, making a mental note to send her that blue gown she'd looked so spectacular in. "I wasn't expecting you up today. Is Erik here, too?"

"He's coming tomorrow. I just couldn't wait to hang out here. It's so fabulous, isn't it?" She touched Allie's shoulder. "You staying the week?"

"Oh, no." She shook her head. No way could she stay among so many memories of her days and nights with Jonas. It was time to go back to New York and start fresh. Learn from her mistakes with him and do better going forward. Wasn't that what dating was about? Finding who was right, who was wrong, what kind of partner you were and what kind of partner you needed.

It was just that at twenty-eight, she was obviously a slow learner. And Jonas had seemed so promising...

Maybe there was still hope, still issues they could work out together. Except they'd always come up against the geographical distance. And his money would always be an issue. Allie hadn't realized how much work she still had to do to come to terms with her father's desertion of the family for a better life. It would be easier to date someone who didn't represent everything she always felt she wasn't.

"You're staying at least tonight, though?"

"Actually, I was planning to catch a bus in a couple of hours." The second she spoke she realized she'd much rather hang out there with Sandra.

"Nonsense. I'm here now. I brought us dinner. There is enough alcohol in this house to float the U.S. Navy, and I think we should put a dent in it. You with me?"

Allie wiped her dusty hands on her jeans, smiling. She'd just figured out what was different about Sandra. She looked happy. Really happy. Sparkles-shooting-out-of-her happy.

Erik. Things must be going well for them.

"You're on. Let me shower off the grime and I'll join you. On the beach?"

Sandra shuddered. "I don't do bugs. In the nice screened-in porch, maybe."

"See you in ten."

She showered and threw on tight pink shorts and an outrageously busy floral top, feeling much more human. Sandra was the kind of woman who could listen and offer advice. She'd grown up poor, and seemed to be doing fine with Erik. Plus she knew Jonas.

Downstairs, out on the porch, Sandra was spreading one of the painted white tables with a picnic of chicken wings, pasta salad, marinated broccoli, peaches and miniature cupcakes in various flavors.

"Yum. That looks fabulous."

"You think that looks fabulous, look at this." She held up a bottle of champagne. "Taittinger Comtes de Champagne, 1995. This stuff goes for *beaucoup* bucks, baby. We are so having it."

"Do you think we should?" Allie was more surprised that Sandra knew the bottle was a good one—even the year?—than that she was suggesting they drink it.

"Erik said to help ourselves to whatever." She untwisted the wire cage. "This was in the refrigerator, therefore I am doing so."

"How did you know about the vintage?"

"My parents loved Taittinger champagne."

"In Southie?" She wrinkled her nose. "Sorry, that burst out. I know you—"

"In Greens Farms, Connecticut. An exquisitely wealthy community on Long Island Sound. I grew up there, the daughter of gazillionaires."

Allie's heart sank. So Sandra and Erik were cut from the same cloth. "But you said…"

"I lied." She poured the bubbly into two flutes, tipping them so the foam would settle faster.

"Why?"

Sandra handed her a glass, her smile tinged with sympathy. "Honey, I think you know."

Allie gaped at her, feeling betrayed. "Jonas told you."

"Cheers." Sandra took a sip and closed her eyes ecstatically. "Oh baby, that is almost better than sex."

Allie followed suit, hardly tasting a thing.

"He told me in general terms under intense pressure. And only after I finally told him my story, which has more details you get to hear later." She pulled out a chair. "Have a seat."

Allie sat numbly. "You hadn't told Jonas before?"

"Nope. Now I've told him and Erik and you. Because I have discovered something important that everyone should know, but which took me over thirty years to figure out. And I am passing this wisdom along to you, my sister." She passed Allie a plate. "Have a chicken wing."

"That's it?" she said incredulously. "'Have a chicken wing'?"

Sandra snorted. "It is that I don't give a rat's ass what anyone thinks of me except the people I love."

"The people you love." Allie was slowly starting to get what Sandra was saying. "Because those are the people—"

"Who must accept me as I am. If they don't…" She hoisted her champagne glass. "Screw 'em. You and I, my darling Allie, have cared too much what the wrong people think. If we want to be happy, we have to go out there and grab our men by the balls and yank until they…what the hell am I saying?"

Allie giggled and reached for the bottle. "I have no idea, but it sounded intriguing. More champagne?"

"Absolutely. You know what's so ironic?"

Allie finished pouring. "No, Sandra, what is so ironic?"

"I started this whole thing just wanting Erik for his money."

"But you grew up with tons."

"My parents cut me off when I was seventeen."

"No kidding." Allie sat there, astounded. She'd spent her whole life making sure she never prized a man for his wealth, and here was Sandra, whom she liked and respected, saying exactly the opposite. "Were you trying to get money from Jonas, too?"

"Yes, but I actually liked Jonas."

Allie nearly snorted champagne. Since she didn't, she drank more. "You know, this keeps tasting better."

"Doesn't it?" Sandra topped off their glasses. "I have a great idea. Let's see how long that keeps happening."

"So you started just wanting Erik's money, but then…" She knew, but she was curious if Sandra would admit it.

"And then I did something incredibly stupid." She dropped her gaze, took a deep breath. "I—"

"Fell in love with him."

Sandra's head jerked up. "How did you know?"

"Ha! It's right up there." Allie pointed over her head, then clenched and unclenched her fingers. "Flashing pink neon."

"Damn." Sandra drained a third of her glass. "So my delicious power play, my fabulous manipulation of the poor innocent man, officially backfired. And it gets worse."

"Wait, how?"

Sandra sighed. "I don't even want to admit how pathetically low I've fallen."

"That bad?"

"I can hardly admit it." She made a face, as if she'd eaten something foul. "I want him to love me for me."

"Oh my God, you're right." Allie kept her face deadpan. "That is horrifying. You are totally screwed."

Sandra burst into giggles. "You need to drink more. You are hilarious."

"You mean now? Okay." Allie half finished her champagne and held it out for more when Sandra offered. "So, now what? You marry him and live happily ever after?"

"*Marry* him? You have to be kidding me." She poured unsteadily, nearly sloshing champagne over the top of Allie's glass. "Men like Erik don't want to get married. He's playing at love. He will keep me around until I start looking old and then he'll trade me in for a younger model."

"No." Allie shook her head. "That's other women. He wants to get married. I bet he asks you."

"Well, I don't know if *I* want to get married."

"Ha!" Allie gestured with her glass. She could see right through Sandra. "You're just putting on your tough act."

"What about you?" Sandra looked at her shrewdly. "Would you marry Jonas?"

"*Marry* him? I barely *know* him." Her voice was an unpleasant shriek.

"Oh, I see." Sandra jerked her eyes to a space above Allie's head and pointed. "Hey, look! Flashing neon!"

"No, no. No, not me. Besides, I made him hate me." For some reason that made her giggle. But then everything was getting funnier by the minute. "Because of how freaked out I was by his money."

"You have to get over that. In fact, you should *enjoy* that. You should drink this champagne that costs a hundred fifty per bottle and say, 'Thank you, gods on Olympus, for bringing me this man who is filthy rich enough to give me endless ambrosia.'"

"Except we're stealing it."

"Only somewhat." Sandra lifted her chin. "They definitely owe us for mental trauma."

"You know, I should have told Jonas sooner." Allie whacked her forehead. "I should have—"

"What, been a different person? You can't be."

"No, you're right!" She nodded enthusiastically. "Once I met Jonas I should have gone back in time and been born into an upper-class family! Why didn't I think of that?"

"No, no, no." Sandra ruined her stern lecture with a giggle she couldn't hold back. "Our only mistake was in thinking of our lives as something that had to be kept secret."

"Amen, sister." Allie stood unsteadily and addressed her congregation of one. "You and I are not our pasts. We accept their roles in shaping us but we won't let them rule us anymore."

Sandra stood opposite her, equally unsteadily. "Nor will we let men rule what we say or do or feel."

"We are whole whether we're with them or alone."

"No more hiding."

"No more lies or cover-up."

"Someone doesn't like who we are?" Sandra signaled Allie to join her. They opened their mouths and shouted together.

"Screw 'em!"

A noise made them both turn abruptly. Allie nearly overbalanced.

Standing in the doorway, laughing at them much harder than was polite, were Jonas and Erik.

CHAPTER FIFTEEN

SANDRA FOUGHT DOWN PANIC, her giddy buzz nearly gone. Had Erik heard her all but admit she was in love with him? That she'd been after his money? God, she hoped not.

No, he couldn't have. He wouldn't be laughing.

"How long have you been standing there?" she demanded.

"Long enough to realize that we are evil oppressors and you like good champagne." Erik walked toward her, his blue eyes still amused, dressed in a blue polo shirt that matched them and black shorts. Sandra wanted to retreat to the other side of the room. The emotions this man brought up in her couldn't be healthy. Deep desire, growing love, fear, vulnerability and anger that he was making her feel all that. She'd probably have a heart attack.

Allie straightened resolutely. "We were thirsty. And didn't think you'd mind."

"It was my idea." Sandra sent Allie a look of gratitude. Sweet kid. With a little straightening out she'd be good for Jonas. Though what had started out as a pep talk for Allie had turned into one for Sandra, too. She was glad she'd come up early. She was clear on what she wanted now. Clear about what she had to do.

Erik put his arm around her and gestured grandly to Allie. *"Il mio champagne è il tuo champagne, mio amore."*

Sandra rolled her eyes, reluctantly impressed. Spanish, French and now Italian? "Language dropper."

He tightened his arm around her. "Come for a walk with me?"

"I don't do walks." She let him kiss her on the cheek, and smiled at him because she simply had to.

"Then come lie down with me," he murmured.

"A walk sounds great, thank you, Erik," she said loudly. In a case of spectacular timing, a gust of wind and a boom of thunder let them know any walk undertaken at that hour would be a wet one. "Or maybe we'll stay right here."

"Allie?" Jonas stood stiffly in the doorway. Sandra glanced at

Allie, who was standing almost as stiffly, and her heart squeezed. Those two needed to be alone.

"Erik, we should—"

"Will you come to the cottage?" Jonas glanced briefly at the gathering storm. "We can probably just make it before it pours. Unless you'd rather I go stand outside with a long metal pole pointed toward the clouds."

"No, you don't need to do that. I'll come." She grabbed the bottle of champagne, only about a third full by now. "But I'm bringing fortification."

"That's not enough to fortify a kitten." Erik dropped his arm from Sandra's shoulders.

"It'll do." Allie stopped opposite Sandra to surprise her with a warm hug on her way out.

"Good luck, honey," Sandra whispered.

"You, too," Allie whispered back. Then she winked, hoisted the bottle and crossed to Jonas with bearing worthy of a queen.

"Hey." Erik had reappeared next to Sandra holding out another bottle. "Just in case?"

"Thanks, this is fine." Allie grinned and followed Jonas out of the kitchen.

"Holy mother of God." Sandra whistled silently, eyeing the bottle. "What do you do, bathe in this stuff?"

"Mmm, want to?"

"I might. I'll tell you when it's safe to ask me." She had one more secret. One last one that she hadn't planned to tell him, ever. But the conversation with Allie had changed her mind. If she wanted him to love the real her, then he needed to know what she was capable of.

"When it's safe?" He swallowed comically. "Uh…"

"So, Erik." She turned to face him, took hold of his collar and stood very, very close. "Would you like to stay down here, or go upstairs?"

His eyes started glazing. "Hmblerwog."

"Upstairs? I thought so." She took a step back, pulling him after her.

"What about glasses?" He held up the bottle.

"Glasses?" Sandra turned around at the bottom of the stairs so she wouldn't trip going up backward. "I thought we were bathing in it."

"Right. Right, I forgot."

"We'll drink from the bottle. Or from—" she ran her tongue over her mouth "—other places."

Erik barely saved himself from tripping. "Don't *do* that."

Sandra giggled, leading him up, thinking how she'd first seen him from these stairs, how she'd been surprised by his appearance, expecting aggressive virility and instead finding this sweet, sexy man.

Whose hands were currently making a very thorough exploration of the movements of her gluteal muscles as she climbed the stairs.

Naughty boy.

She loved him that way, every way. If he loved her that way, as well, would that be enough? Could she invest her heart and soul into this man and risk being ultimately cast aside for his next conquest? Life was so much safer when she had all her lovely barriers to hide behind.

But yes, she could. People did it all the time. Normal, healthy people. If she wanted any chance to be happy she'd have to take that risk, too.

She reached the landing, marched down the hall to Erik's bedroom, yanked down her shorts and kicked them off. Pulled her shirt over her head and threw it across the room.

Erik stood frozen in the doorway, clutching the bottle of champagne, watching her.

Off came her bra. Off came her panties. She stood naked in front of him.

"You." She pointed to the overstuffed chair in the corner of the room, then put her arm down since her hand was trembling. "Sit there and listen to me."

He stayed where he was for an instant, trying to read her face. What he saw must have convinced him this wasn't a game because he nodded, put the champagne on the dresser and crossed obediently to sit. "Okay, Sandra. What's this about?"

"I initially started this game with you because I wanted you to fall in love with me."

"Okay. Well, it worked," he said quietly.

"Yes, but I wanted that because I..." She took a breath and made herself continue, wrapping her arms across her chest, her eyes to the floor. "I wanted your money. I was tired of being alone and struggling, and you seemed like a nice guy, and you have plenty."

"I see." He spoke gently; she was too nervous to look up. "You said 'wanted.' Does that mean you want more than my money now?"

She looked up, then, and it was suddenly easy to talk. "Yes."

A spark of hope lit his face. "How much more, Sandra?"

She unwound her arms, stood naked before him. "All of it," she whispered.

The spark grew into a blaze. Erik got up from the chair and lunged toward her.

"I'll give you all of it, baby."

Sandra burst into giggles. "Eek! Help! Pervert attack!"

"Not the first time, won't be the last." He picked her up as if she weighed fifty pounds and swung her onto the bed.

She lay back, laughter subsiding, waiting for him to undress.

His shirt was off, landing with a swish. His shorts were off. Landing with a clunk.

Sandra blinked. *Clunk?* She lifted her head. "What was that? Rocks in your pocket?"

Erik chuckled harder than she would have thought the lame joke merited. "Actually, yes."

"Aww, you were out collecting beach stuff?"

"Nope." He picked up the shorts and fished in the pocket. "Out buying them."

"*Buying* rocks?" She sank disgustedly onto the pillow, staring straight up. "You rich people are too much."

"I'd really like to show you my totally cool rocks."

"Uh, yeah, sure." She rolled her eyes at the ceiling. "That would be super."

"Okay, I will. After I—"

"Get your rocks—" she turned and smiled sweetly "—off?"

"That was bad." Naked, with a condom on, he dived on top of her, making her squeal again. She welcomed him into her arms, absorbing the broad masculine feel of his body on hers.

And then it was just too silly to put off telling him any longer. "Erik."

"Yes? God, you feel good." He shifted over her, matching them up. Legs, pelvis, torso.

"Listen, I want to—"

"You have the most gorgeous skin, Sandra." He kissed her shoulder, her cheek, her forehead.

"Thank you." She gathered her courage again. "Erik, I—"

"And your breasts are works of art." He showed her with his mouth his deep love of art.

"Thank you. I'm trying—"

"I want to make love to you all—"

"For God's sake, Erik, I'm trying to tell you I love you. Will you *shut up?*"

He froze in shock, staring down at her.

They both burst out laughing. Then stopped at the same moment.

"Sandra." Erik kissed her as if he was never ever going to stop, which she bloody well hoped he wouldn't.

The kisses turned hot and hotter, then he was sliding inside her, arms tight around her, making her feel adored, not confined.

This was what it was like, then, loving and being loved. Something she'd been after all her life, often without realizing it. This was safety, not risk, this incredible connection, making love to each other on a level of intimacy she'd never experienced. Knowing unconditional love for the first time in her life.

If only it could last forever.

Careful, Sandra. Nothing lasts forever. At least not for you.

She blocked the worrisome thoughts and relaxed into the slow, beautiful pace of their lovemaking, a pace that inevitably sped up when their mutual arousal demanded it.

And then she was clutching him, not holding him, he was

plunging not sliding, and she was panting and straining for the climax that hung just out of reach until he changed his angle, making her lift her hips higher. And then, yes, there was the wonderful onrushing ecstasy that burst over her.

Yet through it all, the ultimate surrender, she was always aware of the man in her arms, always aware of them in this together, aware of his pleasure and climax as well as her own.

So different.

Then the gradual slowing of his breathing, the husky tone of his voice when he whispered her name. The deep sigh of contentment that relaxed him, and the echo of hers.

"Sandra."

"Mmm?" She couldn't be bothered to form an actual word.

"I want to show you those rocks now."

Her peaceful face wrinkled into disbelief. He could not be serious. "Now?"

"Yeah. They're great. I got five of them."

"Five rocks."

"Uh-huh." He pulled out of her and got up to get rid of the condom.

Sandra lay on the bed, glaring at its wrought iron foot. Rocks. For crying out loud, *this* was the guy she had to fall in love with?

A smile curved her lips and she stretched her arms deliciously over her head.

Apparently.

"Here." He sat on the bed, reached for his stupid rocks. "But I'm only giving them to you because I love you."

"Sure, okay." She struggled to sit up.

And froze.

Velvet box. Man holding it out to her. Deep love in his eyes. Rocks.

"Oh my God, Erik." She grabbed at the sheet, then realized she was instinctively trying to cover herself, and made her hand stay still. "What have you done?"

"I told you. Bought rocks." He spoke lightly, but his eyes were anxious, vulnerable. "They're for you."

He opened the box. A ring. She couldn't quite believe it until she saw it, sitting right there. A tiny part of her had still been thinking he might have a special box of rare and expensive minerals.

But no. These were diamonds, four of them, flanking a spectacular sapphire.

Five rocks.

"I've been looking for you all my life, Sandra. Half the time I didn't know it. More than half. But I've found you now, and it would make my life truly complete if you'd agree to share it." He slid from the bed and got down on his knees, which meant only his head showed over the top of the mattress. She would have giggled, except his beautiful face was so sincere, and so solemn. Her lovely, sweet Erik, truly hers now, for the rest of her life.

"Sandra McKinley, will you marry me? And yes, money comes with the deal. Because I don't want you alone and struggling, either."

"Yes, Erik. Yes, I will marry you." She touched his face tenderly, happy tears spilling over onto her cheeks. "But I swear I'd take you even if you didn't have a cent."

CHAPTER SIXTEEN

"OKAY." ALLIE STEPPED into the cottage and turned to face Jonas. Rain had blackened his hair and tamped down his curls and was running in droplets down from his temples. His blue eyes were searching. She held up the champagne. "Let's kill this bottle."

He lifted his eyebrows. "Any left?"

"Not much. Got any more?"

"Not of that stuff." He took the bottle from her and strode over to the refrigerator, and took out another champagne, an outrageously expensive one. "Looks like if we want any more, we'll have to make do with this."

"Oh, for—" She glared at him. "Don't you do *anything* like normal people?"

"Um, actually." He winked at her, suggestively, looking sexier than any man had a right to. "Yes."

"Oh. Well. That." Allie found herself smiling at him, when she should be staying strong and letting him know what was what. All of which was a little fuzzy at the moment.

"Jonas." She drew herself up tall. "I want you to know that I really don't care about your money."

"Good." He took down two flutes from the cabinet and poured out the rest of the Taittinger, a full glass for each of them, which under the circumstances was plenty. "I only care about money in that it makes life easy and comfortable, and I can afford to be generous."

"Oh. Well, yes. I meant that your money isn't the issue for me."

"No?" He turned, holding the glasses.

"No. *I* was the issue for me. I mean, I'm sorry I didn't tell you about my life and my dad sooner. I shouldn't have been ashamed of—"

"No." He brought the glasses over and handed her one. "That's not the issue."

"No?"

"No. *I* was the issue. I didn't understand how important it was that you *did* tell me. It was a big risk for you, a huge show of trust in me. I took it the opposite way, and I was wrong."

"Oh. So…" She frowned at him. "What's the issue?"

"As far as I'm concerned, Allie, there isn't one." He leaned in to kiss her, a slow, sweet kiss that made her heart rise up and threaten to spill over like champagne poured too quickly.

Allie looked up into his handsome face, so close in the dimming light, completely undone. "Oh my goodness."

"Yes." He held her gaze, and this time she felt totally at ease. He could look inside her and see whatever he wanted. "I agree."

"With what?"

"What you said."

"What did I say?"

"You said—" he took her champagne, set it on the kitchen table "—that we are really, really good together, and that after this somewhat bumpy start, we should be thinking about getting serious."

Allie put a hand to her chest. "I said that?"

"Uh-huh." He drew her into his arms, bending her back in the crook of his elbow, and kissed her until she became somehow disconnected from the planes and right angles of her regular life.

"Wait, wait." She pressed a finger to his lips to stop his next kiss. "There is an issue. I just remembered it."

"What?"

She pointed between them. "Boston, you, New York, me. You have a job and I just accepted one."

"What job?"

Allie looked at him in concern. "The one I was just offered."

"No, *I* don't have a job."

Her eyes shot wide. "You don't have a job?"

"I submitted my resignation, effective immediately." He drew her close, his hand at the back of her head, kissing her temple and ear. "Right after they fired me."

Allie drew back again. "They *fired* you?"

"I told them what I thought." He chuckled and took her hands. "You and Sandra were right. Telling the truth is very freeing."

"So...so..." Allie was unable to take the next logical step.

"So I'm not anchored in Boston." He started kissing each of her fingers. "Though it would be the best place for me to start a new company. You can decide what you want to do."

She managed to tear her eyes away from his lips on her skin. "Well I mean it's not really a decision. I accepted the other job. I start a week from today."

"Or..." He took her hands and clasped them at the back of his neck, moving her flush against him.

"Or what?" she whispered.

"Or you can call them up and say 'sorry, I got a better offer.'"

Allie moved back from his descending mouth. "Okay, but...I haven't gotten one yet."

"Give me a minute."

"Oh." Her voice sounded very small. Butterflies invaded her stomach in enormous quantities and fluttered up a tornado. She had no idea what to expect, but she had a feeling it was going to be big.

"Allie McDonald, I am offering you my condo to move into, to see how it goes for us until we decide to buy our own house."

"You want to—" Her mouth dropped open. "Our own *house? What?*"

"Hmm." He frowned. "That didn't go over so well, huh."

"No, I'm just. Wow. I mean, I didn't expect—" She broke off and clasped her hands to her cheeks, trying to take it all in. Jonas smiled, a faint curving of his beautiful lips that warmed his eyes and made her feel he absolutely adored her, and that maybe the idea didn't seem quite as crazy as it was. "Do I have to give you an answer now?"

"No." He lowered his mouth half an inch from hers. "There's more."

"Uh-oh," she whispered. "Will I like this?"

His lips grazed hers. "I have no idea."

"Go on."

"Both of us will be trying to start new businesses. My place is paid for, and yes, as hideous as you are going to think this sounds, I can cover expenses while you get on your feet and—"

"No." She drew back, shaking her head emphatically. "No, I can't let you—"

His first kiss shut her up. His second kiss made her incapable of speaking. He dazzled and dazed her with his mouth. If they were really starting a new relationship she'd have to watch that or he'd get his way every time. "Let me finish, Allie."

"Mmm."

"Here's the deal. I will make a ledger and put down every expense. If we break up, you owe me every penny back. If we get married, it's our money anyway, and a moot point."

"Married." She gasped.

"Oops?" He looked at her quizzically. "Did I leave out that part?"

"Jonas!" She shoved him, laughing, feeling her face flushing, joy filling her. She had to be nearly as nuts as he was.

"Hey." He hauled her back against him, grinning. "I would not ask you to move in with me just to try things out. This would be a serious commitment."

"But we're not ready for that." She shook her head. "Are you even in love with me?"

He grimaced, squeezing his eyes shut. "Did I forget that part, too?"

Allie threw up her hands. "That's it. You're hopeless."

One blue eye opened. "Did I mention Erik and I decided not to sell the house?"

She turned her back on him, her hand raised. "Stop talking. Stop now. You're making me completely nuts."

"Okay." Strong arms lifted her and turned her back around. "No more talking."

There was no more talking for a long time. Neither of them said a word as he led her up the stairs. They undressed each other and slid into the bed they'd started the whole crazy relationship in, only this time instead of pushing him out, Allie welcomed him to her. Their lovemaking would be different this time. With one word, she could be starting a whole new life with this man. They could belong to each other for the rest of their lives.

The realization spurred her to new boldness, entirely different from the false security the costumes had given her. She took the lead, taking his already-erect penis into her mouth, tasting him for the first time, discovering how much he loved her tongue and lips teasing and giving him pleasure.

When she couldn't wait any longer, she straddled him, taking him deep inside her, showing him with her movements and sounds how much he was turning her on, watching the excitement he got from her arousal.

Their bodies communicated perfectly, shifting, giving, taking. Allie was no longer afraid to meet his eyes, no longer embarrassed or inhibited by his wanting to watch her nakedness or her pleasure. She was the woman he wanted there with him, even knowing all of her secrets.

Close to coming, she planted her hands on either side of his shoulders and rocked her pelvis forward, rubbing her clitoris against his pelvic bone until her moans let Jonas know she was ready. He grabbed her hips, thrusting hard as her orgasm started, reaching his own climax when she was still in the throes of hers.

Allie slumped down on top of him, totally spent. For a minute or two she lay across his chest, letting her breathing slow, listening to the beating of his heart. Then she lifted her head and met his eyes, which were as full of his feelings as she knew hers were.

And she knew they were true and lasting and real.

"I love you, Jonas."

His mouth spread in that wonderful smile that turned her heart upside down. "And I love you, Allie. I want to live with you and get the chance to see your beautiful face every day. I want to be there for you in whatever way you need me while you pursue a career that matters to you. I want to laugh with you all day and make love to you every night."

"Oh, Jonas."

"Wow." He blinked, looking surprised and pleased. "I think I got it right that time."

"It was perfect." She kissed his chest, trailed her finger along his collarbone, hardly able to take in that they were no longer looking at pain and sadness and parting, but a long life together. "With you I feel more like myself than with anyone else. I have given you more of myself than anyone else. You bring out the best parts of me and tolerate the worst. I am deeply touched that my future career means so much to you, and I would be honored to live with you and help you with yours, as well."

"Sweetheart. Allie." His arms tightened around her, his voice husky. "You feel okay deciding all this now? I know it's soon."

She sighed. "I suppose I should reserve the right to panic. But right now I feel so sure and strong that I can't imagine I'll change my mind."

Jonas grinned and started stroking her hair. "So, um, you'll bring the Cleopatra outfit, right?"

She giggled at his eagerness, giddy at all the plans they were making, all those they still had to make. "You bet."

"It's funny. In our first email exchange I told you a secret I'd never told anyone, about wanting to start my own company. Now we've told each other all our secrets." His hand stopped stroking and he looked slightly sick. "Um. Haven't we?"

"Uh, well…" Allie bit her lip in fake concern. "There's the body in my basement…"

"Oh, no." Jonas clapped his hand to his forehead. "I knew it."

"No, no more secrets." Allie kissed him, kissed him again, rolled with him when he moved them over so he was on top. She wrapped her arms around his neck, gazing at him adoringly. "With you I have nothing to hide."

* * * * *